AMAZING ADITI

Memories aren't the only things that linger

RR Cherla

notionpress.com

INDIA · SINGAPORE · MALAYSIA

ISBN 979-8-89415-984-3

Dedication

To family and friends

Contents

Prologue

With its blend of old-world charm and bustling modern life, Pune held a secret tucked away in one of its quieter upmarket neighbourhoods – a private rehabilitation centre surrounded by well-manicured lawns.

The absence of signage and the building's exterior conveyed the impression of a well-to-do private residence with several outhouses and annexes. The solid doors and windows functioned as a barrier not just to muffle external noise but also to contain the clamour within.

On a bright morning, a luxury SUV drove up to the centre's porch. Inside the vehicle, a woman handed a sealed package to her driver. Without a word but with a clear understanding of the package's significance, the driver stepped out and briskly walked into the building.

The rehab centre lobby was a bubble of calm. Sunlight streamed through large windows, falling on the plush sofas and the reception desk, where a young receptionist multitasked, a phone cradled between her shoulder and ear. The driver approached, clearing his throat to announce his presence.

"Madam has sent this," he said tersely, placing the package on the desk. His voice carried slight irritation, born of the early hour and the task at hand.

The receptionist, momentarily placing her caller on hold, turned her attention to him. "Who is this for?" she asked.

The driver nodded towards the package. "The name and room number are there. Just read it," he said, his impatience thinly veiled.

The receptionist gave him a tight-lipped glare as she checked the package. "Oh, it's for room number 18," she said, then looked up just in time to see the driver walking away. She sighed and beckoned Manju, one of the attendants.

"Manju, take this to room number 18," she said, passing the package to him.

Manju hesitated, a flicker of apprehension crossing his face. "18? That's the violent one. They are all in the recreation hall now. From whom is this?"

"Does it matter? A lady sent it over with her driver; they've just left," the receptionist replied, nodding towards the entrance. "It could be the person who comes to see number 18 once in a while."

As Manju made his way through the corridors of the rehab centre, the sounds of everyday life became more pronounced. Muffled screams and yells seeped out from the rooms, increasing in volume as he advanced.

He reached the recreation hall where inmates were engaged in various activities, some playing board games, others sitting silently, lost in thought. One inmate sat isolated from the others, her dishevelled appearance marking her out. A nurse sat nearby, listening intently as the inmate animatedly explained something.

Manju approached cautiously, offering the package. "Madam, you had a visitor," he said.

The inmate's reaction was immediate and startling. She snatched the package, her movements quick and sharp. Manju stepped back, a mixture of relief and apprehension on his face as he watched her tear into the package.

She pulled out the contents of the package and scanned them, a complex play of emotions on her face as she did so.

Having completed his task, Manju turned to leave and ran into a senior nurse. Unable to contain his curiosity and the question that had been bothering him for days, he asked her, "Sister, why is number 18 always so angry? What's her story?"

The nurse looked at him, her face a mask of professional fatigue. "I look like your grandmother or what, to tell you stories?" she snapped, her arms laden with files. "Get back to work! I have all these case sheets to fill."

PART 1

Memories

1

"Ee Sala Cup Namde"

As the sun began its descent, casting an amber glow over Bengaluru, UB Towers stood like a beacon of sharp ambition against the city's bustling backdrop, its glass façade mirroring the changing sky.

On the bustling Vittal Mallya Road below, the usual cacophony of honking cars, chattering pedestrians, shoppers, revellers and pub crawlers provided a lively contrast to the serene skies above.

Perched high within this urban monolith on the 14th floor, the Zyke offices were a hive of creative fervour. The open-plan workspace, with its minimalist design and pops of vibrant colour from the latest handbag collections, buzzed with the energy of its predominantly young, female workforce. Amid the sleek workstations and casually strewn prototypes, the air was thick with the scent of fresh leather.

On the wall behind the reception, the Zyke logo, with its distinctive "Z", boldly declared the brand's identity and ethos.

At the heart of this orchestrated chaos was Ajay Rawal, the forty-five-year-old CEO. He had just wrapped up a Town Hall where he presented the quarterly results. The stellar performance had left the hall buzzing with applause and optimism.

"Alright, team, remember, we're only as good as our last collection. Let's make the next quarter even better!" Ajay called out to his team. "But for now, it's celebration time."

Ajay strode across the office to his desk, exchanging high-fives with a few young designers whose eyes lit up.

Approaching his secretary Priya, he announced, "Plan for the celebrations tomorrow, Priya, and invite the city's top retailers."

"Done, boss," Priya responded.

"I need to head out now. I've got my book-reading event today," Ajay said, taking a final sip from his coffee cup.

Priya smiled, her gaze still fixed on her task. "All the best, Ajay. I want a signed copy." She reached for her phone and added, "Let me call your driver. You had better hurry if you don't want to be late for your book launch. Traffic's a nightmare today, with the crucial RCB-CSK IPL match on at Chinnaswamy Stadium later."

"*Ee sala cup namde!*" Ajay exclaimed, echoing the RCB fans' rallying cry in Kannada.

"Do you really believe that?" Priya shot back, her face a mix of frustration and scepticism, the typical RCB fan expression.

As Ajay made his way to the elevator, a spontaneous round of "Goodbye" and "See you tomorrow" echoed around him.

As he entered the elevator, the office's hustle and bustle faded away, affording Ajay a quiet moment to ponder the upcoming event. As the doors opened at street level, Ajay was greeted by the lobby's expansive elegance, emblematic of the luxury and space UB City was known for.

Stepping out into the early evening, the warm embrace of Bengaluru's air was immediate. Ajay paused, taking a moment to appreciate the city he now called home, before making his way to the sleek car that awaited him.

2

Reflections

The fading light bathed the opulent, gated, serene environment of Royale Woods, Bengaluru, in a soft glow, casting long shadows on the residents who had gathered near the clubhouse.

The atmosphere was electric inside the clubhouse, with about thirty guests assembled for a book-reading event, a testament to the community's vibrant cultural life. The backdrop of the stage was a banner showcasing the book *Reflections* by Ajay Rawal, setting the stage for an evening of literary exploration.

Ajay sat on the podium alongside the interviewer, Saumya Rao. A former political analyst with a leading national daily and now a respected columnist, Saumya had also published a couple of novels. Her transition to the literary world brought a unique depth to her interviews with authors.

Ajay's athletic build, smart attire and the distinguished streaks of grey in his hair painted the picture of a man who had navigated life's challenges with grace.

As the session neared its end, Saumya smiled at Ajay, "Thank you, Ajay, for reading aloud those thought-provoking passages from *Reflections*. It was fascinating."

Ajay responded with a gracious nod. "Thank you, Saumya."

Saumya's curiosity was piqued. "Ajay, you are the busy CEO of a major lifestyle company. When did you find the time to write a book?"

Ajay's answer revealed a journey marked by perseverance and passion. "I have written these stories over several years. *Silver in the Dust,* the first story, was penned during my college years, while my most recent one emerged earlier this year – we are talking a gap of almost twenty-five years!"

"That's a long period of time," Saumya remarked.

"Yes, the challenge was finding and collating all the stories I had written over the years. Some were on paper, others on old laptops and pen drives, and a few scattered across blogs in cyberspace! I must also thank my wife Shehnaz for her help," Ajay said, his eyes finding Shehnaz, seated in the front row, her characteristic poise and elegance intact. She acknowledged his words with a gentle smile, her pride in his accomplishments evident.

Saumya concluded the session by holding up a copy of *Reflections.* "The book is available here for sale at a great discount. Get your copy signed by the author."

Turning to Ajay, she said, "It is of great pride that one of our residents is not only a top corporate honcho but also a gifted writer. Thank you so much, Ajay."

The audience responded with hearty applause, and as Ajay and Saumya stepped off the podium, many approached Ajay, eager to discuss his book.

3

Blast From the Past

The evening settled softly over Royale Woods as Ajay and Shehnaz walked back to their villa. Their home welcomed them back, a sanctuary of space, art and comfort, a silent testament to their life's journey together.

They sat comfortably in their living room, surrounded by quiet and tasteful luxury, reflecting on the evening's event. "That went pretty well, don't you think?" Ajay broke the silence, a hint of satisfaction in his voice.

"Yes, it was lovely. The Residents Association did a good job organising it," Shehnaz responded, her mind already ticking through the list of things she needed to do next.

The maid interrupted their conversation and informed them that dinner was ready. The moment the maid stepped out, the shrill ring of Ajay's phone sliced through the silence. He picked up with a brisk "Hello."

On the other end, a voice teased through the static. "Is this Ajay Rawal?"

"Yes, who is calling?" Ajay's brow furrowed slightly, his tone curious as well as impatient.

"Guess!" The caller's voice was a playful lilt, stirring a memory not quite reached.

Ajay glanced at Shehnaz, who returned his look with a questioning raise of her eyebrows. "Huh? Who is this?" he pressed.

"Take a guess, yaar," the voice insisted.

Now irked, Ajay warned, "Tell me your name, or I am going to cut the call."

"Wait, wait. It's Carol D'Souza. Fergusson College, class of 1998!"

The name hit him like a wave, leaving a brief stunned silence.

Then he rallied. "Oh my God! Carol!" Ajay exclaimed, his irritation vanishing and replaced by excitement as he covered the receiver and turned to Shehnaz. "Carol D'Souza, my classmate from Fergusson College."

Back on the phone, his voice brimmed with enthusiasm. "Great to hear from you, Carol, after all these years! How have you been?"

Carol chatted away even as Shehnaz's interest waned. "All good. I'm based in Mumbai. You are back in India, I hear. In Bengaluru. With family?"

"Yes, we moved back to India last year. My daughter is studying, and my son is working in the US. My wife Shehnaz is a psychologist, and she is here with me. Shall I put you on speaker, Carol?"

"Yes, of course, it will be lovely to talk to your wife, too," Carol responded.

Once on speaker, Ajay made the introduction. "Carol, Shehnaz is with me. Shehnaz, Carol is my classmate and one of our gang."

"Hi, Shehnaz. Nice to talk to you." Carol's voice filled the room.

"Hi, Carol. Likewise. I have heard of this college gang of yours," Shehnaz responded.

"Yeah, we were quite a notorious bunch," Carol reminisced.

"Not me; you guys were the wild ones. I was the straight arrow," Ajay joked.

"Yeah, right." Carol laughed along with Ajay and Shehnaz.

"So, Carol, what about your family?" Ajay ventured.

"A daughter working in Mumbai," came Carol's reply.

"Husband?" Ajay asked, a hint of hesitation in his voice.

"Divorced. Long ago," Carol stated matter-of-factly.

"Sorry to hear that." Ajay's apology was automatic.

"Why sorry? Congratulations *bol,* yaar!" Carol's laughter rang clear and infectious.

"Divorce has been a new beginning for me. I'm now running my third start-up," Carol continued, sounding proud and content.

"That's great, Carol," Shehnaz chimed in.

"But enough of all this. I called a couple of times earlier this evening," Carol's voice hinted at the business at hand.

"Oh. I was at a book reading. My recently published collection of short stories," Ajay mentioned with casual pride.

"Wow, nice. Listen, next month, we have the twenty-fifth reunion of our 1998 Fergusson College batch in Pune. I am one of the organisers. You and Shehnaz must attend. It's on 25 August. Save the date," Carol's voice was insistent.

"That's great, Carol, twenty-five years. Wow. I'm not sure if we can make it, though, overseas travel coming up. Shehnaz is busy, too," Ajay said.

"Don't give me all that, Ajay; it's twenty-five years, a milestone. Shehnaz, please convince him," Carol coaxed.

Shehnaz, uncertain, looked to Ajay, silently seeking his lead.

"Okay, let me discuss it with Shehnaz and get back to you," Ajay said, non-committal.

"Ajay, it's decided. You two are coming! The whole gang will be there: Viru, Prakash, Nitin, Seema," Carol declared triumphantly.

Ajay couldn't help but laugh, the idea slowly growing on him. "Do I have a choice now? Well, it will be nice to see you and the rest."

"It will be fun, I promise. The morning after, our gang is planning to walk through college, go to the canteen for bun wada and chai, and later, to *Vaishali* for lunch," Carol planned out loud.

"Wow! All our hangouts!" Ajay sounded genuinely excited now.

"I will call off now; I have to make a few more calls. Bye, Ajay and Shehnaz."

Post-call, the room still buzzed from the excitement of the reunion news. Ajay turned to Shehnaz with a grin, "*Eh, kya bolti tu? Pune next month?*"

"No, Ajay. It's your friends and reunion. I'll get bored. What will I do there?"

Ajay, not missing a beat and now in full charm mode, replied, "*Ghoomenge, nachenge, aish karenge, aur kya?*"

"Stop it!" Shehnaz couldn't help but laugh, even as she set her terms. "I'll come if we combine Pune and Mumbai; meet my sister."

"Deal. Let's eat now," Ajay quickly conceded, eager to move past the negotiation and any additional conditions.

Shehnaz leaned in, saying, "Tell me something about this famous gang of yours. And who the hell is this Vaishali?"

"Vaishali? She is my ex, yaar," he joked, the name stirring a trove of memories from his college days.

Shehnaz's sceptical look prompted Ajay to clarify with a twinkle in his eye, "No, it's a popular hangout place on FC – Fergusson College Road. It's world-famous in Pune!"

Their moment was interrupted by the ringing of Ajay's phone once more. "Yes, Carol?" he answered, still chuckling from their last exchange.

Listening, Ajay nodded as Carol spoke, "It's *Reflections*. Stories I had written over twenty-five years." He listened further, a smile playing on his lips.

"I will send you the Amazon link right away. Thanks, bye," Ajay said, wrapping up the conversation.

Hanging up, he turned to Shehnaz, a gleam in his eye. "Carol wants batchmates to buy my book! Reunions are good for sales, she says!"

"That's nice of her; every little bit helps, doesn't it?" Shehnaz replied, finding Carol's enthusiasm sweet.

Ajay looked at the lovely woman beside him. Shehnaz, he thought with pride, not for the first time. Ajay couldn't help but wonder at his good fortune. How did the scrawny and nerdy kid from college end up with a girl like her?

"I knew the studious types would become successful and rich men," she would often joke. Ajay knew his forte was numbers and financial data, a talent not exactly famed for igniting romantic flames!

He fondly recalled their awkward first date, back when he had cleared his Chartered Accountancy exams at the first attempt and was making his mark at one of the Big Four firms. Throughout their first date, he had rambled on about EBITDA, asset turnover, free cash flows and amortization. She, ever smiling, had never appeared bored or exasperated even for a moment. Why she had agreed to see him again would remain one of the unsolved mysteries of the universe for him.

At twenty-three, Shehnaz's allure had been undeniable, turning heads wherever she went. Two decades later, her charisma remained just as captivating. Her hair cascaded to her shoulders beautifully, enhancing the appeal of her captivating eyes that sparkled with intensity. She had an admirable mind and an ability to spar with him, teasing and taunting him.

Her profound empathy and compassion had established her as a distinguished psychologist and a revered mentor for CXOs.

Shehnaz was everything a man wanted, and Ajay was happy to be that man.

4

Down Memory Lane

One month had swiftly passed since Ajay and Shehnaz's conversation with Carol, and now they found themselves in Pune, the city awakening vibrant memories for Ajay. The crisp morning air greeted them as they exited the brand-new terminal of Pune's Lohegaon Airport.

Shehnaz's sister had thoughtfully arranged their transportation, ensuring a visit to Mumbai was on the itinerary. The car, driven by Ajit Shinde, awaited them, ready to whisk them away to their first stop in Pune.

Ajay expressed his gratitude, touched by the gesture. "Nice of your sister to send her car and driver from Mumbai."

Shehnaz laughed, "She's just making sure we visit her in Mumbai. And Shinde is from Pune, so he gets to see his family, too."

As they settled into the car, the driver inquired about their first destination. Shehnaz instructed him to take them to the JW Marriott, where they were booked, but Ajay, his heart set on reliving the past, had other plans.

"Wait. Take us to Fergusson College Road first," he instructed, a childlike excitement in his voice.

Shehnaz protested gently, reminding him of their schedule, "Why now? Aren't we going there tomorrow with the gang? I have some work to finish."

"We have all day today. I just want to have a quick look at FC Road and the joints there," Ajay explained, convincing her to indulge him in this detour.

Half an hour later, as they turned onto the bustling street that was Fergusson College Road, Ajay could barely recognise it. The once-familiar laid-back street was now lined with new retail stores, cafes and eateries; the vibe was still youthful, but the scenery had changed. Parked two-wheelers and pedestrians encroached upon the road.

Ajay's initial disbelief gave way to acceptance as Shehnaz gently reminded him, "Ajay, the road was bound to change in twenty-five years, don't you think?"

Overcome by nostalgia, Ajay asked Shinde to slow down as they passed landmarks that sparked vivid memories. "That's the boys' hostel gate!" he exclaimed, pointing out various places – the Main Gate of the college, the girls' hostel, and Vaishali, their cherished hangout spot.

As they drove past the iconic arch announcing Fergusson College, Ajay was swept up in a wave of nostalgia. Pune was a city once defined by its academic institutions and salubrious climate. During his time here, Fergusson College Road, Shivajinagar and the Deccan Gymkhana area felt like they were trapped in amber – frozen in the pre-Independence era, an epoch in which Fergusson College had played a pivotal role.

Run by the Deccan Education Society, Fergusson College was established in 1885 following a persistent campaign by prominent nationalists and reformers such as Bal Gangadhar Tilak, Vaman Apte and others who recognised the urgent need to modernise the education system. Their goal was to further the cause of reform and create educational institutions aimed at the overall advancement of Indians.

The sprawling stone buildings of the college, grand and historic, stood as sentinels to a bygone era. The leafy pathways meandered through the campus, bearing tales of the days when the city's pace was more measured and reflective of its scholarly spirit. Here, the old Pune was a stark embodiment of tradition and tranquillity.

The contrast was striking as he looked at the busy road leading away from the college. Fergusson College Road had transformed into a pulsing artery of the city. The crowds, the traffic, the buzz of commerce and conversation, all spoke of the new Pune, a city that had grown beyond the tranquil confines of its past, embracing the rush of modernity.

Yet, even with the cacophony of progress resounding in the streets, Fergusson College's stately charm remained untouched.

Ajay couldn't help but feel that the soul of Pune, old and new, was encapsulated right here, between the arches of Fergusson College and the bustling road beyond.

Gazing at the iconic Vaishali restaurant, Ajay's expression turned tender. "Vaishali. O Vaishali," he whispered, his voice tinged with the warmth of reminiscence, as though he had stumbled upon a beloved from years ago.

"You see, Shehnaz," Ajay began, "such is the allure of Vaishali that many of my former classmates from Pune still gather here every Sunday for dosas and filter coffee. Even after all these years, every Sunday! They call themselves the Vaishali Padiks."

Shehnaz, feigning astonishment, responded, "Goodness! Some folks refuse to let go of the past, never grow up!"

Driven by a sense of loyalty, Ajay countered, "You might not feel that way if you'd experienced life here."

5

A Homecoming

Nestled in the Shivajinagar area of Pune, amidst the academic hustle of Pune's most prestigious colleges, Vaishali, the iconic Udupi restaurant, transcends being merely a dining space – it's a cherished chapter in the lives of countless individuals.

For those who've wandered through the leafy lanes of Fergusson College Road, Vaishali isn't just a spot on the map; it's a vault of countless memories, a place where time seems to pause. The emotional connection that the patrons, especially the old-timers and former college students, share with Vaishali is profound.

This connection starkly contrasts with the experience of dining in other parts of Pune. While areas like Camp boast their cosmopolitan vibe, bustling with chic cafes and trendy eateries that cater to the modern palate, they often miss the warmth and intimacy that places like Vaishali offer.

It's this sense of belonging, this unspoken assurance that no matter how many years pass, some things – like your favourite table, the old waiter from your college days who still knows your order by heart, or that special chutney and sambhar only Vaishali gets just right – will remain unchanged.

Started in the 1950s by the late Jagannath B Shetty, a renowned restaurateur, Vashali remains a sanctuary for those yearning for a piece of their past, a reminder of the days spent in the sun-dappled courtyards of colleges in the vicinity.

For the area's residents and old-timers, Vaishali is not just a restaurant; it's a piece of their personal history, a place where every visit feels like a homecoming.

Mutha's Provision Store, next to Vaishali, was still standing after all these years and brought a smile to Ajay's face. The nondescript nook, overshadowed by its renowned neighbour, was the original convenience store, a go-to place for all things sundry. The store also served as a meeting point and communications hub for regulars, relaying messages and parcels with Mumbai-dabbawalla precision!

If Mutha's store seemed to stop time, the absence of the British Council Library and Patil's juice stall marked the passage of it. Roopali and Goodluck Restaurant, a favourite for bun maska, kheema pav and late-night chais were still there, serving as tangible links to his youth.

The Deccan Gymkhana area's lanes and bylanes, with their narrow, shaded paths, lush greenery and diverse old stone houses showcasing colonial, Gothic and traditional Maharashtrian architectures, was another area that exuded an old-world charm.

Tucked away from the hustle of Fergusson College Road and other main thoroughfares, this area reflected Pune's rich intellectual legacy and its status as a centre of learning, art and culture, through street names honouring landmarks, scholars and reformers. Agarkar Road, Prabhat Road and

Bhandarkar Road, with their numerous lanes, not only preserved a traditional aesthetic but also seemed to embrace modern thought. Wandering beneath the green canopy of these lanes, one immediately escaped the din, dust and heat, enveloping oneself in a meditative calm.

Deccan Gymkhana and PYC Hindu Gymkhana, hubs of sporting activity founded in the early 1900s that have nurtured champions, contributed significantly to the vibrancy of the neighbourhood. The daily routine of soccer moms and dads driving their kids back and forth, alongside young athletes rushing to their practices, was and continued to be an integral part of the area's ethos.

"Let's wander through a few lanes tomorrow and soak up the culture," Ajay suggested excitedly. "Sample the street food like Puneri misal. We could also pick up some shrikhand and bhakarwadi from Chitale Bandhu for your sister. And cap it off with chai and bun maska at the Goodluck Café, all in the vicinity!"

Shehnaz, less enthusiastic about local culinary delights and sights than Ajay, wore a sceptical expression and remarked, "For you, culture begins and ends with food! So much talk of culture! Did any of you guys absorb this culture that seems to be oozing from every building and monument in and around your college?" she asked, sarcasm lacing her tone. "It doesn't seem like it."

Responding with a grin, Ajay's retort came quick and light. "That's uncalled for! Our education was well-rounded and a bit more...unconventional. We were on different adventures and busy being the cool ones on campus," he replied. "Especially in our final year in the hostel – we were difficult to reign in."

Shehnaz quipped lightly, "Such a city and college, rich in legacy and learning opportunities, and it seems they were wasted on you guys! Like your parents' money!"

The playful jibes seemed to barely register. Ajay had drifted away, his gaze joyfully fixed on the fading relics of his past as they continued to drive past them.

After allowing him a moment to reminisce, Shehnaz gently reminded him, "Everything is fixed for tomorrow, Ajay." She then instructed Shinde to head to the hotel, ensuring they would have time to settle in, get work out of the way and prepare for the reunion.

As dusk settled over Pune, the JW Marriott stood grandly illuminated. Its portico was a flurry of activity as guests arrived and departed.

Inside their suite, a moment of calm preceded the anticipation of the evening ahead. Ajay, dressed in smart casual attire, gazed out of the window at the overcast sky, which heralded the arrival of evening rains.

Shehnaz broke the silence. "I am ready to leave, Ajay." He turned, and his eyes lit up at the sight of her. Dressed elegantly in a saree, complemented by light jewellery, she embodied grace and beauty.

"Wow, looking great," a beaming Ajay complimented. He caught a whiff of her perfume and remarked, "Lovely scent. Is it new? What is it?"

An amused Shehnaz answered, "Yes, it's new, Chanel."

"Oh!" Ajay responded automatically.

"What 'Oh?'" Shehnaz retorted in an accusing tone. "*I* bought this one for myself because my shameless husband couldn't be bothered to remember our anniversary."

The taunt was lost on Ajay as his senses, triggered by the faint scent, struggled to connect it with a memory that just wouldn't surface from the depths of his brain.

The clap of distant thunder jolted him from his reverie.

Shehnaz, half-joking, half-serious, teased about the impending reunion. "I am sure all your exes at the reunion are going to judge me!"

Ajay, with a playful wink, reassured her, "Let them. And the guys are going to be envious. Let's go. It looks like rain."

As they stepped out to the hotel porch, the evening air was thick with the anticipation of rain. Their chauffeured car pulled up, ready to ferry them to the beginning of a night that promised to bridge the years and bring old friends back together.

6

Echoes of Youth

The evening showers had turned Ajay nostalgic for the city of his past, as he and Shehnaz found themselves trapped in a rain-drenched traffic snarl. "Pune has become so crowded. Not the same vibe at all. Look at this traffic," Ajay remarked, a shadow of remorse clouding his voice for a city that seemed to have morphed beyond recognition.

"I think we are going to be late," said Shehnaz, observing the dense traffic. The driver, Shinde, confirmed their fate with a solemn forecast, "Madam, at least one hour. Rain and weekend traffic."

Faced with the certainty of an extended stay in the confines of the car, Shehnaz seized the moment. "Now that we are stuck here, you might as well tell me something about this famous college gang of yours."

With no further prompting needed, Ajay eagerly started to unravel stories of the friendships that had vividly marked his younger years.

"Our little world spun around a group of five to six of us, a mix of boys and girls, with Carol, Viru – Virendra, Aditi and me forming the core – all of us hostelites," he reminisced.

"Carol had the knack for keeping our spirits high. Never one to bury her head in books, she thrived in a dreamworld of parties, gossip, and the occasional heartthrob," Ajay recounted with a fond chuckle, painting the picture of a young woman whose priorities lay in all things social.

"Viru, with his boyish charm, fancied himself the heartthrob of the campus. Academics were not his stronghold, but his prowess on the football field was unmatched," Ajay shared, his smile widening as he vividly brought to life the image of his friend. "We were known as Jai and Viru."

"And there was me," Ajay continued, "perhaps the quieter one among us, the silent observer, a little awkward and out of depth in social situations."

Shehnaz interjected playfully, "Not the ladies' man you are now?"

"No," Ajay replied, accepting the compliment nonchalantly to tease Shehnaz.

Ajay's narrative then wove in Aditi Joshi, the group's dynamo, her spirit and intellect a beacon that drove them.

"Aditi was our star, a force of nature really, always brimming with confidence and energy. She brought unmatched fun and intelligence to our group. A class topper, she excelled in Economics and Maths, and was always looking to argue about matters she felt passionate about."

This led Ajay to reminisce about a particular memory from college, where the essence of Aditi's intensity and cheekiness came to life.

*

The room buzzed with the restless energy of students settling in, their chatter a prelude to the day's lesson. Professor Mahajan, Head of Department, Economics, at Fergusson College, stood at the front, his patience thinning.

"Class, settle down quickly. We have a lot to cover today. I would like you to meet a new faculty member."

As silence descended, he introduced Dr. Avinash Ranade, a young, affable faculty member, appointed to replace the recently retired Professor Venkatraman. Dr. Ranade, with his easy charm and boy-next-door appeal, nodded in acknowledgement from the front row.

"Dr. Ranade has joined us from Mumbai University. He has a Ph.D. in economics. He is an expert on Banking and Financial Stability. Please give him a warm welcome," Professor Mahajan announced, inviting Dr. Ranade to say a few words.

"I have nothing much to say, really. I am thrilled to be at Fergusson College." Dr. Ranade's voice was clear and resonant, and carried across the room. "I did my schooling at St Vincent's, Pune..." he continued, a statement that bridged his past with his present, revealing his journey back to the city that had shaped his early years.

At the mention of St Vincent's, a ripple of excitement passed through the room. A few "wooos" echoed from corners occupied by ex-students of the school.

Acknowledging this small yet significant connection, Dr. Ranade smiled warmly and said, "Thank you...and I'm happy to return to Pune. I'm looking forward to an engaging semester with you all. Now, I will let Professor Mahajan begin. I, too, am keen to learn from him."

His brief introduction was met with light applause, some students already charmed by his persona.

Professor Mahajan stood at the podium, ready to delve into the intricacies of economic theories with his students.

"The concept of the 'invisible hand' was introduced by Adam Smith to describe how the self-interest of individuals in a market economy can unintentionally promote the

wellbeing of society as a whole," he began, setting the stage for discussion on one of the foundational principles of economics.

No sooner had he started than a hand shot up from among the students. Aditi Joshi, known for her sharp intellect and unyielding curiosity, sought to challenge the day's lesson right from the outset.

Professor Mahajan, recognising the familiar pattern, shook his head in frustration.

"Yes, Ms. Joshi, what is it? I have just started!" he exclaimed, his voice tinged with annoyance and resignation. "Dr. Ranade, meet Aditi Joshi, our class topper," he introduced, with a hint of a smile. "She's the quintessential argumentative Fergussonian!" he added, referencing the college's rich tradition of intellectual discourse and debate.

Dr. Ranade smiled, "Thank you for the warning, Professor Mahajan. I will be prepared."

All eyes in the room then shifted to Aditi, who stood her ground, undeterred by the collective attention.

"Sir, this theory is flawed. The invisible hand theory assumes perfect competition and complete information, which are unrealistic in the real world...." she began, her voice firm and her argument well-founded.

By the end of the hour, Professor Mahajan had furnished a comparative introduction to economic theories, ranging from Classical and Keynesian economics to Monetarism and New Growth theories. He concluded by stating, "...and so, government intervention assumes that the state is impartial and has sufficient information to make the right decisions.

More often than not, these are knee-jerk reactions influenced more by politics than economics."

Pausing for effect, he closed his book on the table, signalling the end of the lecture. "Thank you, class. We are done for the day," he announced.

But the session wasn't quite over for the hapless professor; Aditi Joshi had yet to have her final word.

"Wait, sir, you are wrong about government intervention. Laissez-faire capitalism is..." she interjected, her voice sounding clear as a bell in the classroom.

The room, filled with weary students, including Ajay and Carol, held its head in a blend of anguish and fatigue as it was once again plunged into the academic fervour that Aditi seemed to thrive in.

She was that annoying student, the one who always reminded the teacher about the homework everyone else had hoped would be forgotten.

*

As the car inched forward in the gridlocked traffic, Ajay continued to peel back the layers of Aditi's personality, each anecdote painting the portrait of a spirited woman of diverse talents.

"She was a key member of the college swimming team, too," Ajay said, more than a hint of admiration colouring his tone.

Shehnaz, intrigued by this new revelation, playfully inquired, "Is that why you took up swimming?"

Ajay responded with a light chuckle, "Arre yaar, I learned to swim much later," dismissing the notion while secretly appreciating the connection Shehnaz wove between him and Aditi, his mind wandering back to a vivid memory at a swimming pool.

*

At the aquatic centre, Ajay, Carol and Viru, silent observers from the stands, watched intently as Aditi executed a perfect dive, her form slicing through the water with effortless grace. Her prowess in freestyle swimming was a testament not just to her physical agility but also to her natural talent.

Later, refreshed and radiant, Aditi paused to engage with the boys' swim team on her way to meet her friends. Her presence elicited both respect and admiration.

It was then that Head Coach Cherian spotted Aditi and beckoned her over. "Aditi, I want you at practice. The selections for the All-India Universities meet are next month," he stated, his tone firm.

Aditi's response was a mix of reluctance and pleading. "I don't want to, sir, please. Too much coursework. It's my final year," she replied, hoping to sidestep the commitment.

Coach Cherian wasn't swayed. "Don't say no, Aditi. You have a very good chance to make it," he countered, his belief in her potential unwavering.

Aditi tried to deflect it again, citing her peers' strengths. "Sir, Tasneem from Wadia College has a better 100-metre timing. And our own Anuradha is excellent," she argued, downplaying her abilities.

But Coach Cherian saw through her modesty. "Tasneem's been practicing six months for that timing. You've skipped training all season. With a little practice, you will beat her," he reasoned.

Aditi's resistance crumbled under the weight of her coach's faith. "Sir, please. College-level competitions are good enough for me. I want to concentrate on my studies; I've got some serious post-grad plans," she attempted one last time.

Coach Cherian, however, was resolute. "Aditi, no excuses. I want to see you here every morning. Bye," he concluded, turning to the boys.

*

This narrative brought a new understanding to Shehnaz of the woman who had played such a pivotal role in Ajay's college days.

"Aditi must have been really pretty," Shehnaz mused.

Ajay hesitated and then admitted, "She was a real looker, though she didn't care much for appearances or attire. Always casual, she favoured jeans, kurtas and Kolhapuri chappals."

In Ajay's mind, contrasting images surfaced of Aditi's casual demeanour against her more fashion-conscious peers, highlighting her indifference to superficiality. Her confidence stemmed from a strong self-image and disregard for others' opinions and judgements.

Shehnaz teased Ajay about his recollection. "Jeans, kurtas and Kolhapuris, eh? So much detail about this one girl? I already hate her," she joked.

Ajay laughed off the implied jealousy and retorted, "Hey, you were the one who started talking about her looks!"

Their banter continued, with Shehnaz playfully accusing Ajay of harbouring a college crush.

"No. Our group was all about the fun," said Ajay, sounding sincere about the pure, unadulterated joy of friendship.

"True, a lot of guys chased Aditi, but she couldn't be bothered," Ajay concluded, encapsulating the essence of Aditi Joshi – a woman who, in her youth, was as unconcerned with romantic pursuits as she was about conforming to expectations.

And suddenly, another shard of old memory, a college canteen scene, lodged itself in Ajay's head.

7

Tariq

Ajay, Carol, Aditi and Viru were seated in their usual spot in the college canteen. Viru was busy fending off accusations from some hostel inmates about their missing cigarette packets, helpfully suggesting where they could insert their lit cigarettes.

Aditi was deeply engrossed in her sketchbook, her hands deftly crafting an unflattering caricature of Ajay, much to the amusement of Carol and Viru, and Ajay's mild chagrin.

As the low hum of conversations and laughter spill out from the canteen, a motorbike made its way into the parking area. The rider, Tariq, with a ripped body, donned a T-shirt that accentuated his physique. Something about him suggested he was no stranger to attention.

As the bike came to a halt, Tariq nonchalantly swept his longish hair to the side in a gesture that was both carefree and calculated. He dismounted along with his friend Dipu and strode purposefully towards the canteen.

The tranquillity of the canteen was momentarily disrupted by the arrival of Tariq, renowned across campus for his prowess on and off the athletic field – a true player in every sense.

Carol was quick to note Tariq's presence, hinting at his interest in Aditi. "Look, it's Tariq. I heard he was asking about you, Aditi. He's a decent guy. Did you know he owns a couple of racehorses?"

However, Aditi appeared unfazed, her attention firmly on her sketch. She still managed to quip, "Accha? Wow! Any more useless information I need to know?" Carol made a face and sighed in resignation.

Viru's disdain for Tariq was palpable. "Kai ka decent. Baap ka paisa udatha hai," *he muttered under his breath, to which Carol responded with a sharp rebuke.*

"Tu chup bait, saala. *You are just envious! I believe he has set up an NGO that helps street kids. Not your regular hunk, then."*

Despite Carol's attempts to paint Tariq in a favourable light, Aditi's disinterest was apparent.

His arrival at their table marked a subtle shift in the atmosphere.

"Hi, Aditi. Hi Carol. How are you doing?" Tariq, eyes on Aditi, greeted with a smile that seemed to light up his face.

Carol responded with a warm "Hi," her smile reflecting genuine pleasure at his presence. Aditi, on the other hand, offered a disinterested wave, her attention quickly returning to her sketch.

The boys at the table fell silent, clearly uncomfortable with what they perceived as competition. Tariq's attention was solely on Aditi.

"Can I join you guys for a minute?" he asked, promptly grabbing a chair from the next table and sitting down, not waiting for an answer.

Carol took the opportunity to mention Tariq's NGO efforts, glancing towards Aditi as she did so. "Tariq, I heard about your NGO. Great stuff, yaar," she said.

Tariq's response was humble, "Thanks. I'm doing what I can." He quickly shifted the topic, "Achcha, I am here to invite you all to a party at home. My sister Noor is going to the US to study. Sort of a farewell bash, this Saturday evening at home."

Carol's enthusiasm was instant, "We would love to come, Tariq."

Viru and Ajay, who seldom received party invitations, echoed her sentiment, their "Yes" ringing out in unison.

Tariq's gaze, however, was fixed on Aditi as he extended the invitation to her, "Aditi, see you on Saturday then?"

"No, yaar. My cousin's in town for the weekend. I've got to spend time with her," Aditi declined, her voice devoid of enthusiasm.

"Bring her along. The more the merrier," Tariq suggested, hoping to sway her decision.

Aditi was firm in her response, "No, Tariq. I have not met her in a while." Then she turned to the rest, "You guys go. I am sure it will be fun."

Carol tried to persuade her, "Come on, Aditi! Join us," with all eyes at the table now trained expectantly on her.

Aditi, however, was resolute, "Sorry Tariq, sorry guys. I can't." Then, looking to change the subject, she inquired about his NGO initiative, signalling her appreciation despite her earlier disinterest.

Tariq, seeing an opening again, was eager to share his passion and suggested, "Yes, you should visit our school project in Hadapsar. I could take you there."

Aditi's interest seemed to wane again, "Mmm, maybe sometime."

Tariq, still hopeful, sought confirmation, "So Aditi, is it a yes?"

"Yes? Ah, the party. It is still a no. Sorry," Aditi replied, her focus returning to her sketch.

Tariq, now visibly frustrated, accepted her decision, "Okay, as you wish."

He got up, pushed his chair back a little too roughly and left, leaving behind a table of mixed emotions.

Carol's lament, "Why did you say no? You are such a spoilsport. I can't go without you," was met with Aditi's rationale.

"We don't know his friends. All the drinking, guys hitting on us. It's creepy. It won't be fun like our group parties, with just music, dancing and masti."

Carol, unable to hide her disappointment, turned towards Aditi, her voice tinged with a mix of reprimand and bewilderment, "Tu bhi na, Aditi."

Aditi was steadfast in her conviction. "Nahi yaar, I like to have fun too, just not this kind. You know me, Carol; I don't want to be linked to anyone."

Her words were a gentle reminder of her desire for autonomy, a trait that had always defined her social interactions.

"Tariq seems decent," Carol mentioned, as if suggesting that some connections might be worth exploring, that not all would impinge upon Aditi's fiercely guarded independence.

"You go! Tu ja, phir! Have fun," Aditi said playfully.

Across the table, Viru nudged Ajay, and the two silently made their way through the canteen to the table where Tariq and his friend Dipu were now seated.

The air around Tariq was charged with a mix of irritation and anger, a stark contrast to Viru and Ajay's reverential approach.

"Hi...Hi Tariq. We..." Viru started.

Tariq, already on edge from his recent disappointment, barely masked his irritation.

"Yeah?" he responded, his tone short, signalling his lack of interest in any conversation.

Too caught up in their enthusiasm to notice Tariq's mood, Viru pressed on, "That party on Saturday. What time is it?"

His question opened a chasm of social awkwardness that Ajay immediately widened by asking, "What is the address?"

Ajay actually held a pen and a small notepad, ready to jot down the details of an event that, unbeknownst to him, he was no longer welcome to attend.

Tariq's response was curt, a mixture of disbelief and annoyance colouring his words.

"Huh? Who called you guys? It's a private party for my friends. Fuck off!" His dismissal was accompanied by a threatening wave of his hand that served as the final push for Ajay and Viru to beat a hasty retreat.

Dipu, witnessing the exchange, couldn't hide his surprise.

"How do these losers know of the party?" he asked.

Tariq, with a sigh, revealed the motive behind his seemingly inclusive gesture.

"I thought Aditi would come if her gang was there too, so I called these jokers. She still said no," he explained.

Dipu, sensing Tariq's disappointment, offered a sage piece of advice.

"Hmm, keep trying, beta! Maybe one day...."

*

Shehnaz's laughter filled the car, a cheerful contrast to the steady rhythm of the rain pelting the windows.

"That was so funny. I would have loved to see the look on your face when this Tariq guy told you guys to buzz off!" she exclaimed.

"Yeah, it was embarrassing, alright," Ajay admitted with a smile.

The conversation took a turn as Shehnaz ventured into more personal territory. "So, this Aditi was not into boys? Girls, then?" she asked, her question hanging in the air like a delicate thread of inquiry.

Ajay's mind briefly wandered down a mischievous path, imagining scenarios that made his heart skip. But he swiftly reeled his thoughts back, masking his brief lapse with a hasty and emphatic denial.

"No, no!" he exclaimed, eager to dispel any misconceptions. "It was more about her not finding a connection with any of the college guys. She had set the bar high," he explained.

"Why do you say that?" Shehnaz prodded.

Ajay's mind then travelled back to the tail end of their final semester, a period marked by the culmination of their graduate studies and the looming uncertainties of the future. A time when Aditi's stance on personal connections became a topic of quiet contemplation.

8

Revelation

Outside the canteen, Ajay, Aditi, Carol and Viru found themselves engaged in their daily ritual of sipping tea and eating vada pav, a moment of camaraderie that set the tone for their day.

Aditi, always the one to seek out the pulse of the campus, prompted Carol for the latest news. "Boring day, yaar. What's the gossip, Carol?" she inquired.

"Ms. Kelkar is getting married," Carol revealed, stirring the air with unexpected news.

"Who? From the English Department?" Aditi's interest was sparked. "That's great! She is very pretty; she looks like a student!"

Viru, feigning outrage, chimed in, saying, "What? No! She said she would wait till I graduated. How could you do this to me, Ms. Kelkar?"

Viru's mock outrage at the news elicited laughter from the group. Aditi couldn't resist teasing him, "Don't worry, Viru. Ms. Murthy from History is still single. Only fifty-five years old. It's a perfect match."

"Chup," Viru shot back, then swiftly shifted the focus. "So, when are you girls getting married?"

Viru's query triggered a distressed look from Carol. Aditi, quick to notice, asked, "Carol? What's wrong?"

"Mom's looking out for matches for me. She wants me to get married soon after graduation," Carol revealed.

Aditi's response was immediate and supportive, "That's way too early, yaar. Get a job or study further. Marriage can wait. What do you want to do?" Aditi offered her perspective, genuinely concerned.

Carol's reply came with a hint of resignation. "I am conflicted. You know me, yaar. I want to study. But I want a cushy life, too. Maybe I'll find a rich guy."

Aditi was quick to dismiss the idea, "What, are you mad? Don't even think of it. We must talk about this later. Not here, with these jokers around."

"Yes," Carol agreed, eager to shift the spotlight away from her predicament.

Carol tossed the question back to Viru. "So Viru, what about you? Or have you decided on Ms. Murthy?"

Viru declared with mock pride, "Who wants to be tied down? I am a free bird. No marriage for me."

Aditi scoffed at his swagger, saying, "Good plan because no one will marry a jerk like you."

The playful banter escalated when Viru crumpled a napkin and threw it at Aditi, who deftly swatted it back. Viru then expertly lobbed it straight into the nearby dustbin.

The conversation took a sudden turn towards Ajay, with Carol prodding, "Ajay?"

"What?" Ajay responded, caught off-guard.

"Marriage, duffer. What kind of a girl do you want to marry?" Carol asked.

Ajay was just about to answer, "Well, I..." when Aditi couldn't resist jumping in with a teasing remark, "Ajay? I'm sure he will marry the first girl his mother asks him to. Arranged marriage. Because he's Mamma's boy!"

Ajay's face fell, his hurt showing. Stammering, he tried to defend himself, "No, I...I...will...I will marry someone of my choice. My mom can't force me."

Aditi, realising she may have struck a nerve, softened her tone. "I'm kidding, yaar. Don't be so serious. I'm sure you will get a girlfriend – a hot one!"

Ajay remained quiet, the playful jab from Aditi cutting deeper than he showed.

Attempting to shift the focus, Carol turned to Aditi, "Okay, Ajay. Aditi, what about you? What sort of a guy will you marry?"

All eyes turned expectantly towards Aditi as if awaiting the queen's decree.

"I don't know. I'm not thinking of marriage. It's a long way off," Aditi admitted, her gaze drifting into the distance.

"Arre yaar, I'm not asking you to get married today. Just tell us," Carol urged, eager for a glimpse into Aditi's mind.

Aditi, now reflective, shared her criteria. "Well, he must be mature, self-made — no baap ka paise *types. He must be sensitive, adventurous, and have a good sense of humour. He must have a purpose in life."*

Carol couldn't help but laugh, "Shopping list hai kya? Which planet are you from? Good luck finding one like that."

Aditi quickly dismissed the turn the conversation had taken, "Enough of this silly marriage talk. I only wanted some juicy gossip, not to discuss some drab topic."

With that, she stood up, ready for a change of scene, "I'm off for a swim. Chal, Carol. Bye, guys."

Yet, in her casual departure, Aditi had unwittingly left behind a piece of information – a revelation that would turn out to be crucial, setting the stage for events and developments in the story yet to unfold.

*

As the car wove its way through Pune's rain-drenched streets, Ajay's stories filled the passing minutes. Shehnaz, now privy to a fragment of the rich tapestry of Ajay's college days, felt a deeper connection to the man beside her.

9

Politics, Dirty Politics

In the muted warmth of their car, Shehnaz's curiosity about Aditi continued to unfold. Her gentle teasing about Ajay's fondness for these memories only prompted him to further plumb the depths of his recollections.

"Hmm...she knew what she wanted in a partner," Shehnaz mused.

Ajay was lost in thought and could only offer a thoughtful 'hmm' in agreement. Shehnaz's nudge broke his reverie, urging him to share more about the indomitable spirit that was Aditi.

"Okay, you may as well complete this story since you so obviously cherish memories of her," Shehnaz encouraged, her interest piqued by the layers of Aditi's character.

With a chuckle, Ajay acquiesced, warning Shehnaz, "Don't blame me later. Yes, she was a firebrand, too, this Aditi. Always looking for a cause to fight for," he began, his voice carrying a mix of admiration and nostalgia.

The memory Ajay conjured transported them to a time after the light-hearted debate on marriage outside the college canteen. The sound of angry shouting nearby suddenly pierced the laughter and camaraderie of that moment.

*

Just a short distance from the canteen, the girls' departure was abruptly interrupted by shouting. The voices were angry, the words sharp and threatening, and they were delivered in Marathi.

"*Saala, you better support our candidate for the University Student Council elections!*" The aggressive tone belonged to an unseen voice, but its message was clear and menacing.

Curious and concerned, Aditi and Carol, on their way to the swimming pool, watched a confrontation unfolding.

Three figures, clad in student union colours and emblems, stood imposingly, locked in an argument with Amar Bhide, known around the campus as the UR – University Representative, a title that carried both respect and responsibility.

Aditi, ever the champion of the underdog, couldn't hold back. "Hey, Amar, what's going on?" she called out, her voice cutting through the tension.

Amar approached them, worry etched on his face. "Univ Council election issue. You girls go from here. These guys are goons from outside. It's not safe. Go!" His warning was grave, his concern for their safety evident.

Despite Amar's warning, Aditi moved towards the group, driven by a sense of justice.

Amar confronted the intruders with a defiant stance. "Who are you to tell me what to do?" The goons responded with a menacing step forward.

"If you don't agree, you know what we will do." One of the goons gestured towards some of their allies ominously brandishing hockey sticks a short distance away.

Aditi, now beside Amar and facing the goons, was furious. "What are you guys doing in our college? Get out! We don't want your dirty street politics on campus."

"Who the hell are you?" the lead goon sneered, unaccustomed to being challenged by a girl.

Amar moved protectively in front of Aditi but the situation quickly escalated as a crowd, including Ajay, Viru and Carol, gathered, drawn by the commotion.

Aditi stood her ground, her voice fierce. "None of your goddam business! We have no political party affiliations. Get lost, buggers. We are not scared."

A worried Amar tried to reassure her, "I will deal with these rowdies. You go..."

But Aditi was not to be dissuaded. Her determination sparked a collective courage among the onlookers. Other students joined the fray, their voices uniting in a resounding chant, "GET LOST! GET LOST!"

Sensing the rising fury of the crowd, the goons quickly realised they were outwitted. They beat a hasty retreat but not before hurling the typical bully's taunt, "Bahar aah saala, dikhaenge!"

The students' united front had made it clear: party politics, intimidation and threats had no place in Fergusson.

*

Inside the car, the conversation turned reflective, with Shehnaz expressing admiration. "Wow! A real firebrand, this Aditi."

"Yes, that was her," said Ajay. "On one occasion, Aditi was instrumental in halting the deportation of a foreign student staying in the boy's hostel."

*

Fergusson College and its hostel represented a vibrant blend of students from across India, enriched further by a distinctly international flavour. The rich mix of rural folk and city sophisticates, locals and out-of-towners, the Armed Forces and NRI kids, all created a fertile ground for the exchange of ideas and cultural experiences.

The stone-built hostel blocks, four of them, like other heritage buildings on the campus, held an austere dignity. Each window on its façade was a silent testament to the lives within.

At the entrance to each hostel block stands an imposing gate, reminiscent of the dramatic ones in countless Bollywood films, the kind that one might see swinging open to release a long-incarcerated prisoner into the world, blinking in the daylight and searching for family and cronies. This similarity had turned into a humorous point of reference among the students.

Each corner of the hostel block bore witness to countless escapades and 'jailbreaks' executed by its spirited inhabitants. The walls of these buildings could narrate endless tales ranging from clandestine midnight gatherings to fierce brawls.

The hostels' open courtyards were alive with diverse and spontaneous activities.

Manipuri students masterfully playing Sepak Takraw, mesmerising onlookers, along with peers honing their martial arts skills.

The melodious sound of a flute expertly played by a young virtuoso from Bihar filled the night air as his friends pitched in with folk songs.

Kenyan black belts offering impromptu karate lessons, their towering yet gentle compatriots mastering the art of preparing aromatic African broths, and occasional tensions between international students from rival nations reflecting conflicts from their homelands.

Amidst this rich tapestry of cultures, students from Mauritius added their colourful threads. These students, with *their Indian heritage reflected in their features and uniquely spelt names like Ramgoolam, Seewoosagur, Gungaram and Abdool, brought a distinctive flair to the college. Speaking in Mauritian Creole, a captivating French-based dialect, these foreign yet Indian visitors bridged their Indian origins and Mauritian identity smoothly.*

Their graceful movements to the rhythms of the Sega dance from Mauritius and their prowess at football were not just displays of cultural pride but enchanting enough to weave romantic connections!

Cherished homemade treats vanishing before they could comfort homesick students and epic food battles in the hostel dining hall, featuring hard and sometimes inedible food, with thalis serving as makeshift shields, elevated hostel wackiness to new heights.

*

"How did Aditi help stop the student's deportation?" asked Shehnaz.

Ajay recounted the story with pride and gravity in his voice.

"I don't remember all the details. The African student was an outspoken critic of his country's regime," Ajay began. "He had penned a string of articles for the Pune press that criticised his government's policies. Something to do with foreign military bases in his country.

"The local authorities were pressured by his government to deport him. There were genuine fears," Ajay's voice took on a sombre note, "that he'd be executed if he was sent back to his country under a dictator's rule.

"But Aditi," he said, the admiration evident in his tone, "Aditi and a couple of others from the college, they weren't having any of it. They secured him in the hostel, kept an all-night vigil and thwarted attempts by cops to enter the premises.

"They did all this while they worked out the legal matters, just to make sure he could stay back safely. They bought him time, saved his life, really."

"Wow! That was something! Where is Aditi now? Is she going to make it to the reunion?" she asked, curious about this girl she had heard so much about.

Ajay, navigating the memories as he did the questions, responded thoughtfully, "I didn't see her name on the list. Back then, she had had plans to head to Delhi for her Masters. Her brilliance was evident back then. She..."

Shehnaz interrupted, her tone sharper than usual, "Frankly, Ajay, I'm getting a little tired of hearing about how amazing Aditi was. I'm sure she had her flaws. Everyone does. Was she arrogant?"

Stung by Shehnaz's remark, Ajay realised he had been talking about Aditi the entire way. It was time to do some damage control and put his wife at ease. Maybe revealing Aditi's unflattering side would help. He pondered for a moment before replying, "No, she never really displayed arrogance. Though sometimes her conduct was atypical."

"Like when?" Shehnaz probed, eager to hear more about a character who suddenly seemed larger than life. Despite her annoyance at Ajay's praises of Aditi, she couldn't hide her growing curiosity about the woman who had left such a mark on her husband's past.

10

Right of First Refusal

The college canteen was buzzing more than usual, the air thick with the chatter of students. Aditi and Carol had secured a table amidst the hustle.

Suddenly, Ajay burst onto the scene, his excitement evident. "We won! We beat Wadia College in the football finals," he announced, barely able to contain his joy.

"Wow! After a long time! What was the score?" Aditi couldn't help but share in his excitement.

"One, nil. And guess who scored?" Ajay posed, a grin playing on his lips.

"Viru?" Carol and Aditi guessed together, their voices rising in the noisy canteen.

"Yes!" Ajay confirmed, prompting both girls to break into applause.

The entrance then became the centre of a new commotion as the victorious football team made its entry, their arrival heralded by shouts of "Three cheers to Fergusson." Viru was among them, his presence sparking a wave of cheers.

"Hey, Viru! Hey, Team! Congrats!" Carol shouted across the canteen, her voice carrying over the din.

A beaming Viru made his way over, exchanging celebratory hugs before excusing himself to join the team. The gang watched proudly as the players positioned the trophy at the billing counter, proclaiming victory.

"Hey, isn't that Professor Ranade over there?" Carol's attention shifted to a figure who stood out among the celebrants.

Indeed, Professor Ranade, the new economics teacher, casually dressed in jeans and a T-shirt, was mingling with the students, offering his congratulations.

"Yes. What's he doing in the canteen? Profs never come here. He is quite cool that way, though; I have seen him play football with the guys," Aditi noted, her respect for the professor evident in her voice.

"Yes, he spends a lot of time with students. Not stuck up like the others," Carol agreed.

"Bah! He is just trying to be hip!" Ajay remarked, somewhat cynically.

Professor Ranade's decision to cover the celebration's expenses was met with gratitude. His fist-pumping "Go, Fergusson!" rallied the students around their shared pride in their college.

The celebrations continued around them, but soon, the gang prepared to leave. Carol called the waiter, "Keshav, get the bill," just as a new voice joined their table.

"Hello. Can I join you all?" Professor Ranade, a teacup in hand, was looking for a place at their table.

"Oh. Professor Ranade! Sure, sir." Carol welcomed him warmly.

He settled down, then gestured to the waiter, "Keshav, bill all the football celebrations to me. And tea for all of us here."

Looking around the table, he shared in the collective joy, "Are you guys excited? We won the match! I was at the Wadia grounds. It was a great game."

"Yes, sir, great victory. But we missed it," Aditi replied.

Professor Ranade then shifted the conversation to academics, "Okay. So, how are you all finding my Eco course? Growth and Inflation."

"It's good, sir. But some more examples with an Indian context will help," Aditi suggested constructively.

"Yes, that's a good point. Carol?" he turned to her.

"It's fine, sir. Sometimes, though, it's tough," Carol admitted, reflecting on the challenges of the course.

Ajay shrugged, his attention still partly on the celebrations outside. He regretted never being part of any college sports team, noting that his college chess team never received this adulation.

Professor Ranade said, "I came over to discuss something. I am planning to make the course more engaging," he announced, catching the interest of the table.

"How, sir?" Aditi asked, always eager for anything that might break the monotony of the lectures.

"Rather than me lecturing all the time, I would like students to debate some key topics in class," Professor Ranade shared his innovative approach, which seemed to resonate with Aditi.

"A good idea, sir. Will you be conducting it?" Aditi inquired, imagining the vibrant discussions that could unfold.

"No, it's an all-student affair, with one student moderating and leading the panel. The debate on 'Curbing Inflation' will be next week. And I have decided on the moderator."

As Professor Ranade spoke, Aditi's face lit up with a smile, Carol's eyes filled with dreamy admiration, and Ajay's gaze kept flickering towards Aditi, sensing the anticipation building around the table. The choice of moderator seemed to be a foregone conclusion.

Then came the surprise. "Carol, you will be the moderator and leading it."

Aditi's smile vanished, replaced by a look of shock. Her disappointment was unmistakable, a rare crack in her otherwise composed exterior. Ajay, observant as ever, was the only one to catch the slight shift in Aditi's demeanour, a mixture of surprise and a hint of betrayal.

Carol, overwhelmed, responded, "Oh, me, sir? I have never done it."

"Of course not. No one in the class has. You can do it, Carol. No pressure, but juniors and professors will attend. Maybe even the HOD. It's a good opportunity," Professor Ranade encouraged, trying to assuage her fears.

"Okay, sir, but I will need your help," Carol conceded, her apprehensions clear.

"Of course, Carol. We'll discuss this in more detail tomorrow in class," Professor Ranade reassured, then added as he stood up, "Right, guys. Class beckons. See you."

As he walked away, he reminded them, "Don't pay. The bill is taken care of, thank the football team! Go, Fergusson!"

Aditi remained silent, her enthusiasm noticeably absent as Ajay and Carol responded with a spirited "Go, Fergusson!"

Carol, still flustered, turned to Aditi. "Arre yaar, ye kya musibat, how will I manage? I need your help with that debate thing."

Aditi merely nodded, disappointment simmering beneath her calm exterior.

Later, as the trio got up to leave, Ajay noticed that Aditi's cup sat untouched, the tea cold and a film forming.

*

Back in the present, within the confines of their car, Ajay reflected on the past with insight. "I think she was very angry with Professor Ranade for not considering her," he remarked.

Shehnaz offered a different perspective, her voice soft but certain, "It's just disappointment. She was a class topper, after all."

Ajay, with a lightness in his voice, offered a playful analogy. "Or it was, as we say in corporate deals, right of first refusal!"

Shehnaz laughed at the comparison. "Hah! Carol was a close friend, so Aditi would eventually have been happy for her," she countered.

"I don't know Shehnaz," Ajay ventured. "I heard she had some confrontation with the professor that day. A couple of my friends in the chemistry lab behind the staff room overheard stuff. She seemed upset."

*

Later in the day, fuelled by a sense of unfairness, Aditi made her way to the staff room to meet Professor Ranade.

The conversation that unfolded was a departure from her usual composure, marked by a raw intensity and a dash of immaturity uncharacteristic of her.

"Sir, I don't understand. Why not me as moderator? I am the class topper in economics. It just doesn't make sense," Aditi challenged, her voice tinged with disbelief and entitlement.

Professor Ranade met her gaze, his demeanour calm yet resolute. "Aditi, this isn't about questioning your abilities. It's about giving Carol a chance to grow. We must encourage all students, not just those already confident."

"But that's just it! Shouldn't we reward merit? You have to make me moderator!" Aditi retorted, her frustration evident, her argument veering into the realm of self-interest.

"Leadership is also about lifting others, Aditi. You would do well to understand that. Carol's development is as important as yours. It's about broader growth, not just individual accolades," Professor Ranade explained.

Aditi, however, struggled to contain her disappointment. "So, my efforts get sidelined? That's it?" Her voice rose as she struggled to grasp the situation.

"Aditi, try to see the bigger picture. It's not about sidelining anyone. It's about creating opportunities for all," Professor Ranade responded, his patience wearing thin against her escalating tone.

However, Professor Ranade's resolve remained unshaken; he was determined to give Carol the chance to step up and shine.

Unable to accept the rationale and feeling slighted, Aditi's frustration boiled over. "This is unfair! I am more deserving!" With that, she stormed out of the staff room.

Aditi, often an advocate for fairness and excellence, now found herself conflicted, struggling to balance her ambitions with the collective needs of her peers.

<h1 style="text-align:center">11</h1>

Plans Galore

"So how did you all part after exams? Did you have a big party? Get all sentimental?" Shehnaz's voice danced with a mix of teasing and genuine interest, poking at the veil of nostalgia that seemed to envelop Ajay whenever he spoke of his college days.

Ajay's response was tinged with a hint of melancholy. "No, there was no big bang farewell. We all went our own ways. And lost touch," he admitted.

The memory that Ajay then unfurled was vivid, casting them back to the last day of exams.

*

The examination hall's doors flung open, releasing a torrent of students into the afternoon sun, their relief evident, their joy uncontained.

Ajay, Viru, Carol and Aditi, amid the chaos, found each other with unspoken ease, their steps leading them to the canteen for an impromptu celebration.

"Wait! Let's do Vaishali instead," suggested Viru. "We are done with final exams, after all."

"You clear the exams first," Aditi retorted with a smirk, though the girls eventually agreed to Vaishali.

In a quiet aside, Ajay posed the million-rupee question to Viru, "Tere paas paisa hai kya, Vaishali ke liye?"

"Shhh, damn it!" Viru hissed, casting a nervous glance around. "Does your brain stop working outside the exam hall? Use your head, duffer."

Before the same question could arise in the girls' minds, Viru swiftly steered the conversation to exams.

"Tough paper. I hope I pass. Thank God we are done with exams and college. No more studies for me," Viru said.

"Tough? That was the easiest paper of them all," Ajay countered, a smirk evident in his voice, prompting Viru's playful accusation, "Saala, you ignored me when I asked you for answers in the hall. Ask me a favour again, fucker!"

"Who copies in an English exam?" taunted Ajay. "Only duffers!"

Carol, in no mood for the boys' silly banter, interjected, "Stop it, you two. College and hostel will shut in a few days. What are your plans after that, guys?"

Ajay outlined his immediate future with a sense of duty. "I'm off to Mumbai. A couple of weeks break and then prep for the CA exams. You, Carol?"

Carol's response was tinged with uncertainty, "Mumbai, then Goa. Mom wants me to come back home. Plans uncertain, yaar. Study? Join Dad? Not sure. Mom and aunts are again talking of marriage." Her glance towards Aditi carried a silent plea for guidance.

"Don't rush into anything, Carol. Think about what we discussed," Aditi advised, her tone firm yet supportive.

Curiosity stirred, Viru jumped in, "What did you two discuss?"

Aditi, with a dismissive wave, shut him down. "Viru, you need not know everything we girls discuss."

Unfazed, Viru shifted the conversation, "Some boring girl's talk anyways, right? Hey, let's go to Goa for a holiday, guys. We can stay at Carol's place, save on acco."

Ajay chimed in with a grin, "And food and booze and entertainment."

"Freeloaders. Shameless guys. Next, you will want her parents to adopt the two of you," Aditi teased.

"What's the use of friends in Goa if you can't pile on? What's your plan after college, Aditi?" Ajay redirected the banter.

Carol answered for her, admiration in her voice, "Madam is all sorted. She's off to Delhi soon, has got admission in St. Stephen's, what do you know?"

"Yeah, but I'm keeping my fingers crossed. You can never be sure till the last minute," Aditi responded.

"So, when do you leave? We want a party before you go, okay? And give me all your music and posters," Viru requested, already looking forward to the party.

"Give him your old clothes too, Aditi." Ajay joked, pushing the teasing a bit further.

"Ajay, stop!" Carol interjected, her voice a mix of amusement and exasperation.

Viru, not one to let the jibe go unanswered, swung his leg at Ajay, who easily dodged it.

Amid their chatter, Prakash Kulkarni, a familiar face from the boys' hostel, stumbled up to them. His comfort with the boys was evident in his easy banter, but he kept a cautious distance from the girls, his glances fleeting and filled with unease.

"Oi, yeda hai kya re?" *Prakash teased, directing his jest solely at the boys, careful not to lock eyes with the girls.*

Viru retorted with equal jest, "Tu yeda hai kya? Yede! Cigarette hai kya re?"

Prakash rebuffed him, "Tu mere sau rupya pehle waapas dede, phukatiya."

Viru's plea took on a note of desperation. "Beedi hai kya re?"

Prakash, eager to take a jab at the girls he had never managed to speak to, remarked, "Besharam, tera hep girlfriends ko poonch na."

Before Prakash could let slip any more potentially offensive remarks, Viru swiftly chased him away.

As the group made their way along Fergusson College Road toward Vaishali, they noticed a strange orange hue in the distance.

"Oh hell!" *Ajay exclaimed.* "We better hurry, or we won't find a place at Vaishali. Look, they are all over."

In addition to the usual crowd, Vaishali and the areas around the college, along Fergusson College Road and in the Deccan Gymkhana vicinity, usually attracted a diverse and transient population and groups.

Two of the groups were particularly noticeable and immediately identifiable. These were the cadets from the National Defence Academy (NDA), located in Khadakwasla on Pune's outskirts, and the predominantly foreign, hippy-esque disciples from the Rajneesh Ashram in Pune's Koregaon Park.

The NDA cadets, in their crisp uniforms and blazers, often sought solace in the city's green spaces, a welcome respite from the Academy's rigourous, stringent regimen. Their formal attire, distinctive short haircuts and tough demeanour were unmistakable.

The occasional admiring looks from college girls only encouraged the gentlemen cadets to march down the road with increased confidence and presence. Cold stares from regulars outside Vaishali were not uncommon, but they wisely avoided confrontations with these highly trained cadets.

In contrast to this disciplined bunch, the mostly white disciples of the Rajneesh Ashram, identifiable by their flowing orange robes and sometimes distant demeanour, were altogether another species.

Before their leader, Bhagwan Shree Rajneesh, became widely known as Osho, rumours about the Ashram's liberal views on sexuality, as preached by the guru, captured the imagination of many locals.

Sometimes, as hordes of disciples descended, the area was awash in a vibrant orange hue, while at the restaurants, patrons jostled for space with these generally peaceful migrant flock. Observing the free-spirited Rajneeshites, onlookers felt a mix of amusement and envy, rather captivated by their Bohemian spirit.

Some of the regulars at Vaishali, typically recent graduates or seniors, would engage with some of the female disciples, later boasting about their exploits with "gori detail." They frequently embellished the facts and were usually met with a "Yeah, right" or "Feku saala."

Ajay and gang had managed to secure a table at Vaishali despite the crowd and long lines. Their practised confidence, charm, and occasional fake birthday celebrations usually secured them a spot ahead of the waiting masses. Of course, they did have to endure icy glares, mild protests and a few muttered curses.

Now seated and relaxed after the exams, with delicious food on the table, the group looked forward to a leisurely sojourn at Vaishali. They hungrily gobbled up the sev dahi batata puris like it was going out of style, and quickly ordered more.

Ajay, still preoccupied with payment even as he stuffed his face, was planning to subtly exit just before the bill arrived.

Meanwhile, Viru, the seasoned campaigner, sparked a conversation with a curious, "So, Aditi, what's your plan after college?"

With plans already in motion, Aditi shared, "It's a couple of months before the St. Stephen's semester starts. I am staying back in Pune."

Puzzled, Ajay asked, "In Pune? After college? Why?"

"My parents are visiting from Hyderabad for a few days. They love Pune and are thinking of buying a place here," Aditi explained, a touch of excitement in her voice.

"Nice," Carol chimed in, always supportive.

"Yeah. And listen, I will be joining Pune City Daily for two months," Aditi added, unveiling more of her post-college plans.

Curious, Carol inquired, "What for?"

"They need an artist to illustrate short stories in their weekend literary supplement. I want to sketch a bit, work with local artists, and hone my skills here," Aditi detailed.

"*That sounds interesting and fun. I will be in Mumbai with my aunt, so let's meet here or in Mumbai,*" *Carol suggested, eager to keep the connection alive.*

"*Yess! Wonderful. I'm glad you're close by, Carol,*" *Aditi responded, reaching for a high-five.*

Seizing the moment, Viru interjected, "*Doesn't anyone want to know what I will do after college? I am starting a business.*"

Ajay couldn't help but burst into laughter, "*Tu? Kaun sa business? Raddi dukan? Chai stall? Moong-phali? Business ka spelling maloom kya, saala?*"

Viru shot back, "*Haan, tera baap bada businessman hai na.*"

"*Teri ma...*" *Ajay started to retort.*

Their barrage of insults and risqué comments flowed unabated, the guys ignoring the girls' exasperated pleas for quiet and the shocked expressions of patrons in the vicinity, some of whom covered their children's ears.

It was only when the restaurant manager threatened to oust the boys that they finally toned it down.

The girls always suspected, with some justification, that these arguments were a clever tactic by the boys to escape and leave the girls to pay the bill.

12

Closet love

As the rain eased, granting a brief respite, the stagnant traffic began to inch forward.

"Shinde, how much longer? Is the traffic jam easing up a bit?" Ajay asked.

"Sir, about fifteen minutes. After this signal, traffic will be smooth," Shinde responded.

"Okay," Ajay acknowledged, settling back into his seat, the information bringing a small measure of relief as they continued their journey through the city's rain-slicked avenues.

Pedestrians and motorcyclists dashed out from their shelters, eager to reach their destinations before another downpour. Street vendors hastily uncovered their goods to recover lost time and sales.

"Laxmi Road!" exclaimed Ajay as Shinde navigated the car through the bustling artery in the heart of the city. The major shopping destination was aglow with decorative lights to mark the bazaar's centenary celebration, its rows of jewellery and clothing stores enhancing the play of colour.

"We used to walk through here during the Ganpati festival to see the colourful pandals and devour prasad by the kilo," Ajay reminisced, recalling the deep-rooted traditions of the festival and street that dated back over a century. "Residents and businesses took pride in their Ganesh pandals and stalls. Dagaduseth Halwai's Ganpati Temple was always a major attraction," he mused, highlighting the temple as one of Pune's more revered sites, symbolic of the enthusiasm with which the festival is celebrated in the city.

"Ganpati visarjan days were the best; they were full of festivity and dancing in the streets. The Ganpati dances!" Ajay recalled.

"Is that where you picked up all your vigorous Govinda dance moves?" Shehnaz asked, an amused expression on her face.

Captivated by the vibrancy and riot of colours outside, Shehnaz said, "Pretty place. And here I thought Fergusson College Road was the only road in Pune, the way you always go on about it!"

Looking out at the food and tea stalls lining the street, Ajay, eager as ever to recapture moments from the past, remarked, "This is perfect weather for garam chai and some bajjis."

Catching Shehnaz's stern look, which seemed to read his thoughts, Ajay swiftly abandoned the idea of stopping for a quick monsoon chai.

They soon left the bustling bazaar street behind, speeding down broader avenues toward the Magarpatta area of the city. The monotonous scene of office complexes and apartment blocks whizzing past prompted Shehnaz to return to Ajay's tale.

"It's quite surprising how your group managed to steer clear of the usual crushes and romances," Shehnaz mused, a note in her voice suggesting she was treading on the edges of a more sensitive subject. "Did you, by any chance, have a crush on Aditi? Your stories seem to have a distinct focus on her," she teased, a slight edge to her voice.

Ajay, caught off-guard by Shehnaz's directness, paused momentarily, contemplating the memories and feelings that swirled around Aditi's image. "Not exactly a crush, but I won't deny that Aditi had such a vibrant personality that one could not..." he began, trailing off, leaving the sentence between them.

Shehnaz, seizing the moment, pressed further with casual insistence, "...that one could not help but fall in love with her?"

"Nooooo! Stop! You are putting words into my mouth," Ajay protested, though his smile betrayed his amusement at the conversation's turn.

Encouraged by Shehnaz's gentle prodding and assurance that a college crush could hardly threaten the foundation of their long-standing marriage, he relented and was about to venture into a more vulnerable admission.

Ajay's heart was suddenly gripped by a longing he hadn't felt in decades, triggered by the floral freshness of the *Chanel Boy* perfume that Shehnaz was wearing.

Aditi never used perfume but always had a fresh scent about her, the delicate afternote of lavender soap. Ajay would often find himself leaning in just a little closer, hoping to catch that familiar scent, investing it with an imagined connection.

Closing his eyes, Ajay took a deep breath, now seeking that familiar and pleasant aroma.

"A penny for your thoughts," Shehnaz said, observing the suddenly silent man beside her.

Ajay wisely decided to keep this particularly vivid memory from his college days to himself. Oversharing could have its perils!

He looked at Shehnaz fondly and smiled, his odd longing quickly fading. He felt immensely grateful that she was his life companion, college crushes, first loves, past fantasies and aromas notwithstanding.

"Well, I'll admit it – I did have a liking for Aditi. I even thought of asking her out. But that never happened," Ajay confessed to Shehnaz.

"There's only so much one can discuss over canteen chais," Shehnaz quipped, a twinkle in her eye. Yet, the question of why Ajay never pursued his feelings for Aditi lingered. "But why did that date not happen?" Shehnaz asked, her curiosity getting the better of her.

Ajay's response was hesitant, a reflection of introspection and perhaps a bit of the pain that came with the memory.

"For multiple reasons, I think. I lacked the courage to ask her. Then, there was the thought that perhaps I was not her type. Also..." he trailed off, the words catching in his throat as he approached a more delicate truth.

Shehnaz, sensing the shift in Ajay's tone, gently pressed for more. "Also, what?" she inquired, her voice soft, offering a space for Ajay to share without judgement.

"There were moments when she'd make me feel small," he admitted, his voice barely above a whisper.

"Are you certain?" Shehnaz asked, her voice softening with concern.

"On several occasions, her remarks left me feeling hurt and...." Ajay started, the memories still sharp, a testament to the impact those days had on him.

And suddenly, he was back at the college canteen, a scene alive with the everyday chaos of student life.

13

'Zee French Feelm'

In the lively atmosphere of the college canteen, amidst the clatter of dishes and the buzz of students unwinding, Ajay and Viru were engaged in a seemingly endless game of matchbox flicking, each trying to land a matchbox in an empty glass at the centre of the table.

Carol, her patience wearing thin at the boys' juvenile entertainment, snatched the matchbox midair with surprising alacrity. "Stop! How can you guys play this silly game all day?" she chastised, rolling her eyes.

Viru, keen to stir things up, asked, "Where's your partner in crime?" as he nodded towards the canteen entrance, anticipating Aditi's arrival.

Carol sighed, "Who, Aditi? Probably driving some professor nuts or arguing with student leaders about elections. She's a hopeless case!" But as if summoned by their conversation, Aditi breezed into the canteen just then, her arrival like a gust of fresh breeze.

"Hey guys! Guess what?" she asked, brimming with excitement.

Viru, quick with a quip, guessed, "Your dad sent you money. You are treating us to lunch at Vaishali."

Aditi rolled her eyes at Viru's attempt at humour, "Your jokes are so stale, Viru."

Carol, curious, leaned in, "What's your great news?"

"I got some passes to Katrina Kapoor's 'Mera Pyar Deewana.' Today, the first day, the one o'clock show," Aditi announced triumphantly.

Carol's surprise was evident, "What? Passes? How?"

"My aunt in Mumbai sent them. Her firm is the media partner," Aditi shared.

Viru, seizing the moment, rallied, "Great. Let's go!"

But Carol remembered their academic obligations, "Arre kya let's go! We have Psycho class in ten minutes."

Aditi, undeterred, proposed rebellion. "Let's bunk it, yaar – boring stuff. We will get the notes later. Chal, Carol."

Carol hesitated but was quickly swayed, "Hmmm...okay. I guess we must see it on the first day and have bragging rights!"

Amidst all the excitement, Ajay was quieter than usual and had been eyeing a poster in the canteen for an entirely different kind of cinematic experience – an award-winning French art film being screened at the Alliance Française.

Hoping to cast himself in a more sensitive and cultured light, he glanced nervously at Aditi before suggesting, "There is an award-winning French art film being screened at the Alliance. Let's go see that..." His voice trailed off, laden with anticipation of her reaction.

Clearly, the mature and sensitive Aditi would prefer an art film over typical Bollywood fare. She would be thrilled to find Ajay shared her tastes and would gleefully accompany him to Alliance, leaving the other two to watch the Hindi film.

Or so Ajay thought.

"Yuck! Watch some drab French art film instead of 'Mera Pyar Deewana?' Never!" Aditi exclaimed with intense disdain.

Viru chimed in, parroting Aditi, to rile Ajay, exclaiming, "Yuck! Yuck! Yuck! Yuck!" sounding like a wounded puppy.

Aditi, deciding then and there, told Ajay, "You go for that since you are not interested in 'Mera Pyar Deewana,' I have only three tickets anyway. Carol and Viru want to see it, so I will take them."

Ajay, feeling sidelined and desperate to be part of the group's plans, began to protest, "But I too want..."

Viru donned an accent he thought was French, mocking Ajay's cultural aspirations, "Azay...You go ala see zee Frenz feeelm! Bonjour madam. Muaah. Muaah." The laughter that followed, though light-hearted, stung Ajay more than he cared to admit.

As the trio prepared to leave, Aditi threw a casual "Ajay, bye. Enjoy the art film" over her shoulder, her words a playful jab but a piercing one nonetheless.

Viru, gleeful at the prospect of an afternoon with the girls, couldn't resist a parting dig once the girls were out of earshot.

"I am going to sit between Aditi and Carol in the theatre. In the dark...muuah!" His idiotic mimicry of a kiss left Ajay feeling even more frustrated.

Impatient with Viru's antics, Carol called out, "Chal, yaar. Time waste mat kar. Ajay, take notes in class, okay?" urging Viru to hurry as they left a dejected and somewhat resentful Ajay behind.

The waiter's arrival, presenting Ajay with the bill to settle, along with a rude reminder, "Bill bharo! Koi paisa nahin diya" was the final indignity.

14

Summer of '98

The rain had eased off, leaving the city streets bathed in a soft afterglow as the traffic finally began to move more freely.

"French film! That 'sensitive Ajay' card did not work!" Shehnaz chuckled, amused by the thought of Ajay being playfully shot down by Aditi.

"You know, she did stuff like that! Maybe she liked to mock me!" Ajay's response was a mix of resignation and a lingering sense of injustice.

Shehnaz, trying to offer a different perspective, suggested, "She probably did not realise how she sounded." Her attempt to smooth over the sharp edges of Ajay's memories was met with silence.

"Is there something else? Did she say something really nasty?" Shehnaz probed further, sensing that Ajay held back more than just anecdotes of playful banter.

Ajay's following words came with a hint of defiance, a spark absent in his earlier reminiscences. "No, but I thought I should return the favour. And so, I did something," he revealed, his voice blending mischief and pride.

"What? Did you insult her publicly? Mock her? A silly prank?" The tone suggested Shehnaz was expecting a tale of juvenile retribution.

"Silly? What do you mean? I was not a pushover in college!" His voice was laced with annoyance.

Shehnaz, taken aback by the intensity of Ajay's reaction, quickly sought to defuse the situation.

"Whoa! Where did that come from? Chill, Ajay. Tell me what you did."

Ajay glanced at his watch, then out of the window, as if gathering his thoughts or perhaps steeling himself to recount the details of his prank.

Eventually, he began to tell a tale of mischief born from a mixture of hurt pride and a desire to assert himself, to remind Aditi and perhaps himself that he was not merely a background character.

"After college, we all scattered," Ajay began. "I moved to Mumbai, Carol took off for Goa, and Viru returned to Nashik. Aditi stayed in Pune, working for a local paper."

Shehnaz nodded, encouraging him to continue.

"I dabbled a bit in writing in college but never mustered the courage to share my writings with others," he admitted.

"And what does this have to do with Aditi?" Shehnaz probed.

"Well," Ajay leaned back, a wistful look crossing his face, "shortly after the final exams, back in '98, I penned my first short story, *Silver in the Dust*. It was a tale of friendship between an elderly beggar woman and a young graduate."

Shehnaz's interest deepened. "And?" she prompted, eager to hear how this piece of Ajay's past connected to Aditi.

Ajay smiled, the memory clear and bright. "I've tweaked it a bit since then, but it remains largely unchanged. It even kicks off my book, *Reflections*."

"Aah, that one. It's one of the best," Shehnaz acknowledged, recognising the story's significance.

"I almost dropped it from the book. But it was my first story ever, and it showcases my evolution as a writer, as I have highlighted in the introduction," Ajay explained.

"So, after college," he continued, "I thought about reaching out to Aditi, seeing if her newspaper might be interested in publishing it. She was the artist for their literary supplement back then, her summer job in Pune while she readied herself for PG at St. Stephen's."

"And?" Shehnaz was fully drawn in now, the story unfolding like the layers of an intriguing novel.

Ajay sighed, the pain of the past dimming the spark of his enthusiasm. "I remembered how Aditi sometimes made me feel overlooked during college. So, I thought, why not have a little fun?"

In a corner of Ajay's mind, a montage of interactions with Aditi played out, each scene underscored by the sting of her words.

*

First, there was the day Aditi, with her sharp wit and artistic talent, decided to capture the essence of their group in caricatures. Ajay remembered how she depicted him: with an exaggerated nose and a comically puzzled expression, a visual reminder of how she saw him.

Then, there was the time the conversation had turned to the future, to marriage and life beyond college. Aditi's comment about him being a "mama's boy" and destined for an arranged marriage had echoed in his head. Her words, perhaps meant in jest, felt like a dismissal of his abilities, relegating him to the role of the classic boy next door, unadventurous and unremarkable.

But the moment that lingered most painfully in Ajay's recollection was the French art movie snub. Aditi's immediate dismissal of Ajay's suggestion that they watch a French arthouse film instead of a Bollywood film, her deeming it "drab" and "pretentious," had stung. It felt as though she hadn't just dismissed the suggestion but also him.

Every comment Aditi made, followed by laughter, seemed to underline her disdain.

*

Ajay smiled, a playful sparkle in his eye masking the hurt from those memories. "I always fancied myself as a best-selling author, so I came up with a *nom de plume* in college – *AK LOUIS*."

Shehnaz, leaning forward with a spark of interest in her eyes, couldn't help but laugh at Ajay's revelation. "AK Louis! Why that name? Like JK Rowling?"

"Well, not exactly," Ajay replied, his grin broadening at the comparison. "It's a convoluted combination of AK-47 and Louis L'Amour, the writer of Westerns. I thought it had a nice ring to it, and it sounded Indian, too, perhaps hailing from Goa or Mumbai. Plus, it sounded badass!"

Shehnaz shook her head, still chuckling. "Okay, AK Louis, get on with the story. This I have to hear."

Ajay took a deep breath and continued, "I decided to submit my short story *Silver in the Dust* to the newspaper as AK Louis, a 28-year-old from Mumbai. I even created a new email address to hide my true identity. Aditi knew nothing of this."

Shehnaz's expression shifted from amusement to surprise. "Devious! I didn't know you had it in you. But exciting!"

"And guess what?" Ajay leaned in, the story taking hold of him as much as it did Shehnaz. "My story got accepted for publication, and Aditi was assigned to create the illustrations for it."

"Alright," Shehnaz said, intrigued. "So, you started corresponding with Aditi under this AK Louis persona?"

"Yes," Ajay confirmed. "We exchanged emails about the story's background and the author's profile. It got quite detailed. And she requested all this information about AK Louis, the supposed author."

"So, you just made it all up?" Shehnaz was both shocked and impressed by the lengths Ajay went to maintain his ruse.

Ajay nodded, a mischievous twinkle in his eye. " I crafted AK Louis' life story based on all those conversations we had in college about ideal partners. You know, mature, self-made, ambitious, sensitive, with a good sense of humour... Aditi always had this distinct idea of a partner, which she talked about a few times. I made AK Louis fit the bill."

Shehnaz's uncertain laughter filled the car.

15

AK Louis, IPS

Ajay's story then unfurled, revealing layers Shehnaz hadn't anticipated.

"AK Louis, IPS," Ajay explained, a hint of pride lacing his voice. "He was a 28-year-old IPS officer from the Maharashtra cadre on deputation to the Intelligence agencies. His work? Delving into intricate matters of internal security."

Shehnaz turned to him, curiosity mixed with disbelief on her face. "Why a police officer?" she asked, trying to piece together Ajay's strategy.

Ajay chuckled, clearly enjoying the recounting of his tale.

"I figured a dash of cloak-and-dagger stuff would add an exciting twist. Plus, I had a neighbour who was not only a well-regarded IPS officer but also tough and highly principled."

Shehnaz frowned, her disapproval apparent. "Hmmm," she murmured, pondering the ethical implications of Ajay's actions.

But Ajay was undeterred, swept up in the momentum of his story. "I also portrayed AK Louis as a mature guy, doting son, committed to supporting the underprivileged," he continued.

"Oh, to match her ideal guy profile!" Shehnaz stated, understanding dawning. "And she fell for that? A smart girl like her?"

Ajay's excitement was apparent as he leaned into his narrative. "The prank was a masterpiece, flawlessly executed," he said, his smile broad.

"It was a con!" Shehnaz countered.

"Our communication unfolded through emails under the façade of AK Louis, complete with a photo. Back then, texting and mobile phones weren't what they are today. Aditi's curiosity was certainly piqued, and she appeared captivated by this AK Louis character. It made the entire exchange enjoyable, I will admit!" Ajay's voice carried a mix of nostalgia and mischief.

"You didn't dare to approach her directly, so you hid behind a fake profile and led her on!" Shehnaz accused, though her voice held more curiosity than anger. "So, when did you finally tell her?"

Ajay paused, the story reaching a pivotal moment. "After a while, I decided to reveal the truth to her. In person. So, donning my AK Louis persona, I informed her that I was coming to Pune for work. I suggested we meet up to discuss the submitted story. Aditi suggested Sheetal for an evening coffee."

"Sheetal? Now, who the hell is Sheetal?" Shehnaz demanded, a bit flustered. "Where do all these girls keep popping up from? Vaishali, Sheetal!"

"Sorry, but there's a Roopali and Amrapali too in the mix," Ajay chimed in, unable to hide his amusement. "Deal with it, Shehnaz."

"Oh, really! Throw in a Lajjo and Alamzeb, and you've got the ensemble from *Heeramandi!* Who is this Sheetal, anyway?"

At Vaishali restaurant, the sunken sit-out area serves as a stage for a delightful blend of eras. It is casual yet intimate. Canopies of green and white striped awnings and umbrellas everywhere, the space was a lush enclave on the bustling Fergusson College Road. Waiters weaved through the tables with practised ease, balancing trays laden with the restaurant's sumptuous dishes.

Young couples, lost in date-night bliss, nestled close at their tables. They whispered sweet nothings, shared desserts, and engaged in intimate exchanges while remaining completely unfazed by the surrounding bustle.

Scattered among these romantics were the veterans of Fergusson College and other regulars, a few extra inches around the midsection. Their tables were rich with laughter; they exchanged stories and expressed regret over missed romantic pursuits and the all-male parties they couldn't persuade even one college girl to attend!

A few devoted waiters, advanced in years yet lively, remnants of their college days, playfully teased the old-timers with a warmth that came from years of familiarity.

"This place is home for us." Patrons and staff seemed to share and convey this sentiment to anyone curious about their unwavering loyalty. The nostalgic atmosphere would be perfectly encapsulated if Billy Joel, a college-time favourite of many older patrons, were crooning *Piano Man* from a corner, echoing the sentiment of the moment… *You've got us feelin' alright.*

Amidst their nostalgic tales, these old-timers still managed a sprightly, roguish glance at passing college girls – a testament to the adage that while the hair may grey, the eyes never age.

Here, in Sheetal, the sit-out section of Vaishali, life slows down just enough for people to savour the moments that matter.

The peculiar lingo of locals in Pune's Shivajinagar and Deccan Gymkhana areas, particularly their seemingly risqué suggestions like *"Think we should try Amrapali? Or maybe do Roopali,"* has been known to offend the sensibilities of outsiders.

For the record, Roopali and Amrapali, along with Vaishali and Sheetal, are sister eateries on Fergusson College Road, each adding to the ensemble with its *apsara* and courtesan-like charm.

"Okay, Ajay, no more digressing. How was your meeting with Aditi at this Sheetal place? Was she angry?" Shehnaz asked, leaning in, eager for the climax of Ajay's tale.

Ajay, however, hesitated, not answering her question directly. "I went to Pune the following week and headed to Sheetal to meet Aditi, and tell her about the prank," he said, his voice trailing off, leaving Shehnaz curious.

*

The evening air in Pune was crisp, filled with the buzz of daily life winding down as Fergusson College Road thrummed with activity. Vaishali restaurant was alive with the chatter of its patrons, its lights casting a warm glow on the pavement outside.

Aditi, with an air of anticipation mingled with nerves, made her way towards the restaurant, her steps hesitant as she adjusted her clothes and hair, trying to present herself well for the meeting that could help unlock the author's mind and gather insights that could enrich the storytelling.

Across the street, in front of the British Council Library, Ajay, hidden partly by the urban camouflage of trees and parked vehicles, watched with bated breath. His heart raced as he caught sight of Aditi approaching from up the road. The moment of confrontation, long imagined and meticulously planned, was finally upon him, yet a wave of uncertainty washed over him.

Inside, Aditi secured a table for two in Sheetal – the lush green compact sit-out area of Vaishali, a spot buzzing with the energy of countless reunions and casual meetings. She sat, her gaze flitting over the crowd, searching for a face she imagined belonged to the enigmatic AK Louis. Every new entry into the restaurant seemed to draw her attention, her anticipation growing with each passing minute.

Ajay, meanwhile, struggled with a tumult of emotions as he crossed Fergusson College Road to the restaurant. His initial resolve wavered under the weight of the impending reveal. Peering through the entrance, he saw Aditi, a lone figure of anticipation, her eyes darting towards the door with each new arrival. The sight tugged at something within him, a mixture of guilt and an inexplicable reluctance to shatter the illusion he had so carefully constructed.

Moments turned to minutes as Ajay stood frozen, caught in the throes of indecision. The thought of Aditi's potential anger and the possibility of disappointment in her eyes became insurmountable barriers. With a heavy heart, he retreated, leaving the warmth of Vaishali and the expectations of Aditi behind.

As Ajay vanished into the anonymity of the Pune evening, Aditi remained, waiting for AK Louis.

*

Back in the present, in their car, Shehnaz's voice cut through Ajay's recollections, filled with disbelief and concern. "Wait, hold on. Are you saying you didn't meet her? You just... just...walked away?"

Ajay nodded. "Yes. The thought of facing Aditi's anger was too daunting."

Shehnaz's reaction reflected the incredulity and disappointment Ajay himself had felt. "What? Seriously! AJAY!! How could you do that? The poor girl!"

"It was not my proudest moment," Ajay conceded.

Shehnaz, still seeking resolution, asked, "Did Carol tell her later? Did someone tell her?"

"No! No! I never told anyone about this prank. Not Carol, not Viru, not anyone. You are the only person who knows this. Not another soul," Ajay revealed dramatically.

A heavy shroud seemed to press down upon Ajay and Shehnaz as they grappled with the weight of the story that had just unfolded.

The driver's voice, announcing their imminent arrival at the reunion venue, did little to dispel the tension.

"*Haan, theek hai,*" Shehnaz replied to Shinde, her voice a mere whisper. The silence stretched on, each second ticking by like an accusation, a reminder of the unresolved past that Ajay had just laid bare.

Finally, Shehnaz broke the silence.

"So, Aditi never knew a prank was played on her. She believed the wonderful AK Louis was real and that he stood her up that evening."

"Yes," Ajay admitted, guilt evident in his voice. "After that evening, I abruptly stopped our correspondence. Aditi reached out by email to AK Louis, questioning his absence, but I did not respond. I deactivated the fake account. I severed contact with our entire group since then, and it wasn't until Carol's call about the reunion last month that we reconnected."

Shehnaz's question was pointed, a mirror to the conscience Ajay seemed to be avoiding. "Did you even think about how she might have felt?"

Ajay's defence came quick. "Shehnaz, honestly, it was a long time back. It was nothing more than a silly prank. Why dwell on it now? Everyone has moved on; it's long forgotten."

Shehnaz fell silent for a beat, her mind wrestling with Ajay's justification and sense of right and wrong. After a moment, she acquiesced, albeit reluctantly.

"Yes. You're right. Twenty-five years is quite a stretch of time. No reason to feel guilty now, I reckon. Forget it."

"Yes. It's fine," Ajay echoed unconvincingly, his gaze drifting to the outside world, perhaps seeking release in the changing scenery. "I think we are almost there. Let's go in there and have a blast. I am so excited!"

As they arrived at the venue, The Royal Citadel Club, an exclusive members-only club on the outskirts of Pune, the rain ceased, leaving in its wake a clear, star-studded sky punctuated by the distant rumble of thunder. Ajay and Shehnaz walked toward the club, their footsteps echoing on the wet pavement.

A night filled with laughter and reminiscences loomed ahead promisingly.

PART 2

Reunion

16

Grand Entry

Ajay and Shehnaz walked through the plush lobby and reception area of The Royal Citadel Club, which was designed to resemble the opulent palaces of the Maratha era.

The walls were adorned with portraits of Maratha rulers and Peshwas. For many decades, Poona had served as the seat of administration of the Maratha Empire, playing a pivotal role in defending India from various invaders, particularly during the 17th and 18th centuries.

A grand portrait of the founder of the Maratha Empire, Chhatrapati Shivaji Maharaj, occupied pride of place opposite the entrance.

The decor included a display of coat of arms and martial implements on the walls, complemented by paintings depicting key battles and forts, celebrating the valour of the Maratha rulers and armies. Ancient maps and paintings showcased the extensive reach of the Maratha Empire, which covered a significant portion of the Indian subcontinent.

The club's General Manager, dressed elegantly in a Kolhapuri silk saree, welcomed Ajay and Shehnaz, and guided them to the Raigad Banquet Hall.

The banquet hall buzzed with an energy unique to gatherings of old friends reuniting after years. As Ajay and

Shehnaz stepped inside, the air was filled with laughter, excited chatter and the soft strains of instrumental music.

Shehnaz nudged Ajay. "Recognise anyone? Carol? Anyone from your gang? Ex-girlfriends?" she teased.

Ajay's gaze swept across the room, a mix of apprehension and anticipation on his face. The distinctive click of heels on the floor heralded someone's approach. It was Carol.

Carol D'Souza possessed a striking and warm beauty. She was clad in a tasteful blue dress that was elegant yet simple. Carol's short hair framed her face in a style that was both practical and chic.

"AJAY!! Good to see you!" she exclaimed, turning her warm gaze to Shehnaz. "You must be Shehnaz. Glad you two could make it."

The reunion was immediate and heartfelt. "Carol! Great to see you. You are looking good! I'm glad to be here. Can't wait to meet everyone," Ajay responded, his excitement evident as they exchanged hugs.

Carol, a member of the club and the host for the evening, guided them further into the room, promising a test of Ajay's memory.

They hadn't moved much further when someone they had just passed hailed Ajay with a teasing *"Kya re hero. Pehchana nahin?"*

The gentleman was in his late forties, and the signs of time were evident in his balding head and the paunch that marked his midsection. Ajay looked at him blankly.

Carol looked on, amused, waiting for Ajay to piece together the puzzle.

Ajay's momentary blankness turned to recognition, and he laughed, embracing the man. *"Oye! Viru saala!"*

"Not bad. *Pehchan liya*," Virendra 'Viru' Patil responded with a chuckle as they shared a warm hug, Ajay keeping an arm around him in camaraderie.

"You look prosperous! *Kidar hai tu aaj kal? Kya kar raha hai?*" Ajay inquired.

Carol chimed in with a revelation that surprised Ajay, "Can you imagine Ajay, our free bird, live-for-the-moment Viru is a file pusher now! A bureaucrat!"

"*Kya? Sachee?* Bureaucrat? I thought you would be running a few bars and casinos in Goa or Las Vegas!" Ajay exclaimed in astonishment.

"Viru, meet my wife, Shehnaz." He made introductions and turned the conversation towards personal updates. "And how about you? Is your wife here…or are you still flying solo?"

With a lowered voice, Carol shared a cheeky insight, "Our free bird in college is a mouse in front of his wife. She has him on a tight leash!"

"*Arre yaar! Kuch bhi!*" Viru protested, but the others' laughter drowned out his objections.

"So Viru, where are you based now?" Ajay inquired, steering the conversation back.

"I am with the Education Department, posted in Nagpur," Viru replied.

"Imagine Viru, and education!" Carol exclaimed, sparking another round of laughter.

"So, I hear you have become some hotshot CEO! And a writer and whatnot!" Viru said, looking at Ajay with a mix of pride and disbelief.

"*Fit dikh raha hai yaar!*" he complimented Ajay. Turning to Shenaz, he added, "You should have seen this bugger in college. Such a nerd."

Ajay retorted with a light-hearted warning to Shehnaz, "Don't believe anything this bugger says. *Bada feku tha college mein!*"

Just then, a pleasant-looking lady approached. "Hey guys, meet my wife, Meenakshi," Viru introduced, leading to a round of greetings and introductions.

As the group's laughter and banter filled the air, Carol, the complete host, reminded them, "Okay, guys, get comfortable. *Daaru* is over there. Please don't fight over it like in college. *Kafi hai!* And no food fights! See you later. I've got to check on the arrangements."

As Ajay navigated the familiar yet transformed landscape of old, a sudden pat on his back momentarily startled him. The voice that followed, loud and unmistakably familiar, sliced through the ambient chatter and music.

"*Yeda hai kya re?*"

The phrase, a relic from their college days, instantly brought a broad smile to Ajay's face as he spun around to meet the gaze of the classmate responsible for the odd question.

"*Pakhia! Yeda hai kya re?*" Ajay shot back, using the phrase with affectionate familiarity. The exchange triggered a burst of laughter, a round of hugs, and a surge of chatter that momentarily drew the attention of those nearby.

Ajay turned to Shehnaz. "Shehnaz, meet Prakash Kulkarni. Mr. '*Yeda hai kya!*' Or, 'Are you mad!' It was his favourite greeting back in college."

The introduction was met with more laughter, resonating with shared history and inside jokes.

Viru chimed in, his tone a mix of amusement and mock exasperation. "He came to my office last week and greeted me that way in front of my juniors! *'Yeda hai kya re!'* I've lost all respect in the office now. Grow up, Pakhia!" His complaint only added to the merriment.

Ajay couldn't resist a playful jab. "*Biwi ko bhi aise bulata hai kya?*" The question spurred fresh laughter, the joy of their reunion filling the air.

The evening unfolded as a montage of moments – Ajay, Viru, Carol and the rest, mingling, laughing and reconnecting with classmates.

At the bar, old friends hugged, raised toasts, and celebrated the years gone by and the paths that had diverged, then converged again here at the reunion.

17

'Yeh Dosti...'

The atmosphere in the reunion hall became electric as Carol stepped up to the podium. Her presence alone commanded attention; she had been the driving force behind the silver jubilee reunion, putting in considerable effort to make it a reality. Meticulously planned and coordinated with her staff, no detail was overlooked, from the invites to the yearbook to the mementoes. Carol had ensured it would be an event to remember.

"Hello! Hello! Quiet, please. Listen, guys!" Carol's voice cut through the chatter with authority and warmth. The room gradually fell silent, anticipation in the air.

"I hope you guys are having a good time," Carol began, her eyes scanning the room filled with faces from the past. A cheer erupted from the crowd, a boisterous affirmation that echoed the sentiment Carol hoped to hear.

"Thank you all for coming to this reunion. We have classmates from the USA, UAE, UK, Mumbai, Delhi, Kolkata and Bengaluru."

A voice rang out from the crowd, "Pune! Pune!" drawing laughter as Carol acknowledged it with a playful, "*Haan, Haan.* Subbu has come from far-off Pune! Give him a round of applause!" There were jeers from the crowd. The exchange, filled with humour and camaraderie, underlined the evening's spirit.

Carol's next proposal brought a hush over the room: "Before dinner, I would like each of you to come up here, introduce your spouses or partners, and tell us what you did after college...and maybe recount a few anecdotes from college. Let the spouses hear all the gory details." The suggestion was met with cheers, and the prospect of sharing their journeys and misadventures sparked excitement.

"And later, the dance floor will be open. We have a young DJ coming. Her name is DJ Gaga," Carol continued, her announcement met with more cheers, particularly from the guys, whose enthusiasm was punctuated by whistles and catcalls.

"The guys haven't changed one bit! Still rowdy and desperate!" Carol exclaimed. "Okay, let's catch up some more and get back up here later."

Carol then pumped up the group with a spirited shout, "Once a Fergussonian..." and held out the microphone to the gathering, which responded with an equally vigorous, "Always a Fergussonian!" The rallying cry of proud alumni.

"Yeh dosti, hum nahin chodenge..." echoed through the room as the band delved into treasured Hindi classics, ushering in a wave of nostalgia. Arm in arm, Ajay and Viru burst into the familiar song, their enthusiasm eclipsing their vocal skills.

Being back among old friends felt wonderfully right.

18

Transitions

As the night wore on, transforming the reunion hall into a cosy enclave filled with the warmth of old friendships, Carol, Ajay, Viru, Prakash, Shehnaz, and another classmate, Nitin, found themselves clustered around a table littered with starters and drinks.

Nitin had always been a unique figure in their college days. His family, deeply entrenched in the city's political scene and real estate business, wielded considerable influence. Despite this, Nitin remained the quiet, strong type, never seeking the limelight but always present as a reliable figure in the background.

A bottle of Old Monk at the centre of the table served as a beacon, the expressly chosen pirate's nectar embodying the spirit and camaraderie of bygone days.

Ajay raised his glass in a toast and yelled, "OMG!"

Confused glances prompted him to clarify, grinning widely, "Old Monk Gang! Here's to the OMG!" His pride in coining the term was evident.

"OMG," the men echoed, enthusiastically joining in the toast.

In the background was the unmistakable and hilarious sound of their classmates attempting to hit the high notes of some old Hindi and English classics.

A Dada Kondke song from their college days, filled with double entendres, was heartily sung in one corner by the more smashed guests. The boys' embellished rendition upped the risqué quotient. In the spirit of the evening, it appeared no one took offence.

As the melody of Marathi cinema's comedy king filled the air, the gentlemen at the table, irresistibly drawn in, started singing along to an old favourite, *"Dagala Lagali Kala."*

Carol leaned over to Shehnaz with a smile, remarking, "Cringe-worthy," thankful that Shehnaz couldn't grasp the Marathi lyrics.

"Do you recall our version of *'Khoya Khoya Chand?'*" Viru inquired, giving Ajay a wink.

"Don't you dare continue!" Carol interjected almost instinctively, raising her voice. "Not one more word!"

Turning to Shehnaz with a look of exasperation, she complained, "These guys have spoiled so many classic Hindi songs for me. I wish there were a way to unhear all of that nonsense."

Pre-empting any chance of a comeback from the boys, Carol deftly redirected the conversation, "Can you believe it's already been twenty-five years? How did time fly so quickly?"

Ajay replied, "We can't wait another twenty-five years for the next reunion. We'll be hobbling around with canes by then!"

Shehnaz, curious about the urban college legends, chimed in, "I'm looking forward to seeing Fergusson College tomorrow. Especially this canteen you all practically lived in. Did you ever actually go to class?" Her question drew a collective chuckle from the group.

With mock solemnity, Ajay admitted, "It's nothing short of a miracle that we graduated."

Viru, with a teasing glint in his eye, playfully undercut Ajay's humility, remarking, "Oh, stop it, Ajay. You'd secretly study and then act all surprised when you aced the exams."

This exchange set the tone for Ajay's reflections on their transformation since college.

"Hardly. But look at you now, Viru, Director – Technical Education. It's wonderful. Back in college, you were the ultimate party animal. *Bevda saala,*" he reminisced.

Carol remarked, "I hope you two don't start with those *ma-baap gaalis* here, like you used to back in the day." Turning to Shehnaz, she added, "You should have heard the filth the hostel boys used to hurl at each other. Straight out of the gutter."

"Our college personas are transient. People change. Look at us now," Ajay interjected.

Carol chimed in, her voice tinged with nostalgia. "True, Ajay. You were such an introvert in college; you hardly spoke to the girls. We were the chatterboxes." She teased, winking, "Not bad, you have landed a wonderful wife – smart and stunning!"

Shehnaz blushed at the compliment, playfully dismissing it with a wave.

Carol's curiosity led her to ask, "Shehnaz, how did the two of you meet? Why did you marry *this* guy?"

Shehnaz responded with mock remorse, "Sometimes, I wonder too! But it's too late now," eliciting the group's laughter.

"And now Ajay is the CEO of a women's lifestyle products company. See how fit he is! Surrounded by pretty women at work, I bet!" Carol continued.

Shehnaz, joining in the jest, remarked, "Tell me about it!"

Ajay protested, "Hey, you two, stop! You just met, and you are already ganging up against me. What happened to old loyalties?"

The conversation then shifted to Carol, with Viru recalling, "And look at Carol. In college, she was the chatterbox and not into academics. Parties, movies, and stuff like that!"

Ajay, impressed, corroborated, "And look at her now, a seasoned entrepreneur. How many successful start-ups have you built, Carol? Three? Four? You are the most enterprising of our lot!"

Carol modestly replied, "This is my third. The IPO will be next year."

Ajay then turned to Nitin. "And Nitin is a successful real-estate developer. He was such a calm guy in college, now a politician in the making, I hear. Assembly or Parliament? BJP? Congress? NCP? Shiv Sena? Which party?"

"Let's not forget the numerous factions! I always find it challenging to grasp the parties, factions, and alliances in Maharashtra," Shehnaz contributed.

Nitin replied with a non-committal shrug. "I am still thinking about it. Not this election, maybe the next. Let's see."

Viru sagely added, "He won't contest. He is a kingmaker."

The mood turned when Ajay inquired about Aditi, their fourth musketeer, wondering about her absence from the reunion and whether she was abroad. All eyes turned to Carol, whose face fell, a shadow of gloom passing over it.

Just then, Viru, Prakash and Nitin, inspired by the alcohol and evening's spirit, got up and joined the singers, their voices adding to the chorus of nostalgia and camaraderie that filled the room.

Finally feeling a sense of privacy with only Shehnaz, Carol and himself at the table, Ajay leaned closer to Carol as he attempted to speak over the music. "So, Carol, where is Aditi?" he inquired.

"Sad story, guys," she finally murmured, her voice barely audible over the swell of singing. "Depressing. I'll tell you later, maybe at dinner or after." Her gaze met Ajay's, earnest and pleading. "Just promise me, this stays between us."

The reunion's joyous atmosphere continued, but Carol's words hung in the air.

19

Truth Be Told

As the reunion crept late into the night, the atmosphere shifted from boisterous revelry to a more subdued, reflective mood. The earlier cacophony of laughter and singing gently faded into the background hum of dinner conversations and the clinking of cutlery.

Gradually, the crowd began to thin out. Goodbyes were said, some reluctant, some cheerful, each accompanied by promises not to let decades pass before the next meeting. Hugs were exchanged, contact information swapped with earnest promises of staying in touch, and laughter echoed in the corridors as people made their way out.

In the dimming light of the nearly empty hall, Ajay, Carol and Shehnaz huddled around a table, with the remnants of their drinks. The hotel staff moved quietly in the background, clearing tables, and signalling the end of a night that had woven a tapestry of emotions and memories for all present.

Ajay broke the silence, the question he had been holding back now finding its voice. "So, Carol, you wanted to tell us about Aditi," he said.

Carol hesitated, the weight of the story she was about to share momentarily anchoring her to the silence. "Sad story. I don't know where to begin," she finally admitted.

"What is it, Carol?" Ajay prompted gently.

Carol took a deep breath, her gaze drifting to a point on the wall. "Remember our earlier conversation about how people transformed post-college? You, Ajay, Viru and I have turned out to be quite a contrast from our college selves," she began, laying the groundwork for what was to come.

Ajay nodded, prompting her to continue.

"Aditi changed, too," Carol said, a note of nostalgia colouring her words. "In college, she was this force of nature – confident, grounded, and never really bothered by what anyone thought. She was always there for me." A brief smile flickered across her face as she remembered. "Without her, I would have gotten into so much trouble. You remember how impulsive I was."

"Yes. You guys had a great friendship," Ajay acknowledged.

Carol's smile faded as she ventured deeper into the story. "I don't know if you remember, Ajay, but Aditi was to join St. Stephen's in Delhi," she mentioned, setting the stage for the pivotal changes in their lives after college.

Ajay nodded, leaning in to catch every word.

"She wanted to stay back in Pune for a bit. I was in Mumbai for a while, so I would visit Pune to meet up with Aditi. She told me she was working on illustrations for the local paper. They were running a series of reader-submitted short stories," Carol continued.

Ajay and Shehnaz listened, the atmosphere around the table thickening with anticipation.

"One time when I visited," Carol said, "she told me she was illustrating an interesting short story for a fascinating author!" Carol's voice trailed off.

Ajay felt a knot form in his stomach. The mention of a story and its author sent a chill down his spine as the prank he had played on Aditi made a return.

Carol was unwittingly hovering around the edges of a long-concealed secret.

Ajay's apprehension grew as she paused, perhaps considering how much more to reveal. "She was in touch with this writer to get some background of the story and something about him for the author profile," Carol said. "This guy was a cop or something. He was part of some agency – CBI or ED or RAW, I don't remember. You know, one of those government agencies."

Ajay and Shehnaz exchanged glances, the implications of Carol's words slowly dawning on them. Carol, meanwhile, seemed oblivious to their reaction, lost in the narrative she was piecing together.

"Where did he live? Pune?" Ajay ventured, his voice a cautious whisper, as if afraid to disturb the unfolding tale.

"No, not Pune. Mumbai. He was from Mumbai," Carol confirmed, her affirmation casting a shadow of realisation over the table.

Silence enveloped them for a moment; each beat stretching out as the significance of Carol's story settled in.

Shehnaz, unable to contain her curiosity, prompted, "Then what happened?"

Carol continued, her gaze distant as if recalling a story from another lifetime. "This guy came across as quite the enigma, a tough character, his police work shrouded in secrecy. To top it off, he was a responsible son who looked after his parents. Aditi seemed captivated by this guy. It almost seemed like she was developing strong feelings for him."

Grasping for straws, Ajay asked, "What was this guy's name?"

Carol's annoyance at the question was clear. "Name? Ajay! What does it matter? How would I remember his name after all these years?" she replied, dismissing the question as inconsequential.

Ajay retreated, chastened. "Of course not. I was just asking," he said, trying to mask his growing apprehension.

Remembering a crucial detail, Carol added, "He was, if I recall correctly, a Catholic. But that's beside the point. Anyway, this was a totally different Aditi. Back in college, she wouldn't spare a glance for even the most handsome and popular guys, but here she was, getting mushy about this older cop from Mumbai."

The story left Ajay reeling, his mind racing to piece together the looming implications of his long-ago prank.

"I wish you could have seen this side of Aditi," Carol remarked sorrowfully.

20

Mushy Stuff

Under the canopy of Vaishali restaurant's sit-out area, with Pune's morning sun casting a gentle warmth over their table, Carol and Aditi engaged in an unusual conversation. The usual buzz of the restaurant enveloped them, but for Aditi, the world seemed to narrow down to the excitement within her.

Carol, ever the romantic and the inquisitor, couldn't help but probe, alight with curiosity. "I have never seen you this excited about a guy! Who is this mystery man from Mumbai?"

Aditi, usually composed and self-assured, seemed transformed. Her eyes sparkled with excitement and wonder as she leaned in closer, her voice taking on an animated tone. "Carol, he's so cool. He has this top-secret job with an Intelligence agency in Mumbai. Very mature and sensitive. You should read his short story. And, you know, he's taking care of his elderly mother. Loves trekking, too."

Carol's eyes widened in surprise, her friend's words painting the picture of a man who seemed almost too perfect to exist outside the pages of a novel. "Seems too good to be true. But this is great, Aditi. I'm so glad you're taking an interest in someone."

Aditi's smile radiated happiness. "This guy is different, Carol. He's not like those conceited, self-absorbed, brainless types."

Unable to resist, Carol leaned in, her voice dropping to a whisper. "Enough! Tell me, how does he look?"

Aditi, a blush creeping up her cheeks, whispered back, "Quite handsome, Carol. Hot! At least in his email profile picture."

Carol's response was a drawn-out "Oooooh!" She was excited and delighted at her friend's burgeoning romance and the mystery of a man who had captured Aditi's heart with just words and a profile picture.

*

Carol resumed her story, her voice a soft echo in the now quieter banquet hall.

"They kept in contact through email for a few weeks," Carol recounted, her eyes lost in thought as she sifted through her memories. "Then, suddenly, Aditi shared that he was coming to Pune for work."

Ajay and Shehnaz, deeply engrossed in Carol's tale, felt their apprehension grow.

The merging narrative brought a sense of foreboding. Shehnaz reached out, her hand finding Ajay's under the table, offering silent support.

"You should have seen how excited she was," Carol added.

*

A couple of kilometres away from Fergusson College, under the canopy of an early morning sky, Pune's Kamala Nehru Park on Dr. Ketkar Road brimmed with the gentle hum of nature and the rhythmic footsteps of its early visitors. Aditi and Carol, on a leisurely stroll, seemed encased in a bubble of joy.

Aditi, her excitement barely contained, shared her thrilling news with Carol. "This AK Louis, that's his name; he is coming to Pune this weekend for work. I am so excited," she said, her eyes sparkling with the prospect of meeting the enigmatic writer and police officer.

Carol responded with a hint of wariness. "What work?" she inquired.

Aditi's reply was laced with intrigue, "I don't know. He said it's classified government stuff. You know he is a police officer with the Intelligence agency. He wants to meet me."

Carol's response was measured, "Hmmm."

Aditi, unable to contain her glee, sought advice. "I am excited, Carol! What should I do?"

Carol, protective and practical, cautioned her friend, "Aditi, be careful. You don't know this guy."

But Aditi brushed off the concern, "Arre. What is the problem, yaar? It's just a meeting. And he is a writer. I am sure he is a nice guy."

Carol laid out her conditions, "Just meet him for coffee. Do not go out for dinner or drinks. And meet him early in the evening. And at Vaishali, where you know the waiters."

Aditi laughed off the precautions, "Arre, what is this? You're talking like he is some underworld don! Or serial killer!"

Carol stood firm. "See, Aditi, I am sure he is a nice guy, and there is no harm in meeting him. But why take chances? Coffee at Vaishali, evening."

Aditi, her spirit undampened, teased Carol for her protective stance, "Look who's talking. Remember how many times I got you out of trouble, saali! I know how to take care of myself. Don't be such a grandmother!"

"Fine, go on then. Have fun," Carol remarked, making a playful grimace. "Let's go for some hot poha and chai at the stall outside."

Spotting a stray in the park, an elated Aditi instinctively crouched to pet it, tenderly murmuring, "Ohhh, puppy, puppppy," while the dog nuzzled against her.

*

Carol, her throat parched from recounting the story, paused to take a deep breath and a sip from the glass of water before her. Ajay and Shehnaz, their expressions a mix of anticipation and apprehension, waited for Carol to continue.

Carol's voice, tinged with regret and reflection, filled the quiet left by the departed revellers. "The day they were to meet, she was so nervous. The concern about her appearance and clothes – it was so odd to see Aditi like that. Crazy over some guy and trying to impress him!" She shook her head, lost in the memory of a day that seemed to spin away from everything they knew about Aditi.

She paused, her gaze distant. "To her, he looked like the strong, mature, and sensitive type – qualities she thought her guy should have." A sad smile played on her lips as she added, "I vaguely remember some discussion about this when we were still in college."

Caught in her thoughts, Carol continued, her voice barely above a whisper, "I tried to warn her. Maybe I should not have let her go! If only…"

Ajay, guilt gnawing at him, stayed quiet. Shehnaz, perceiving the weight of Carol's regret, extended a comforting hand to rest on Carol's arm.

Carol paused reflectively, her expression clouding as she delved into a painful memory.

21

Gloss and Glam

The girls' hostel was located at the southern end – the Vaishali end – of the campus, strategically placed a safe distance from the boys' hostel, which occupied the northern extreme. This proximity to Vaishali made the khatta across from the girls' hostel a favoured spot for idlers who lounged on it, eyeing and making snide remarks about the girls who passed by.

A mere glance from a displeased girl was enough to dissolve the boys' bravado and send them scampering back to the safety of their friends inside Vaishali! Despite their hasty retreat, the boys harboured a persistent belief that the girls, their apparent disinterest notwithstanding, might secretly be appreciating the attention.

Those occupying the khatta, backsides firmly planted at one spot for hours, often found themselves aggressively jostled by fellow students eager to take in the scene, marking a contentious battle for the hottest people-watching real estate in town.

That evening, Aditi's hostel room at Fergusson College was a whirlwind of nervous energy and excitement, a stark contrast to the usual laid-back vibe. Clothes littered the bed, each piece a testament to Aditi's indecision and Carol's growing impatience.

Standing in front of a full-length mirror, Aditi shifted from one foot to the other, assessing her reflection with a critical eye. "How is this top? Too plain?" she queried.

Carol, lounging on a mattress on the floor, looked every bit the picture of exasperation. "Aditi, this is the sixth one you've tried on. They all look fantastic on you. You make anything look good. Just pick one and go yaar," she replied.

Undeterred, Aditi held up another one, her brows furrowed in contemplation. "What about the blue kurta?" she asked, hopeful of a different response.

Losing her patience, Carol retorted, "Wear the one you have on. This is too much. This is not a date. Just coffee. With a guy you haven't even spoken to!"

Ignoring Carol's protests, Aditi continued her pre-meeting ritual, now concerned with makeup. "You think I should wear perfume, lipstick? Do you have yours with you? What colour is it, red?" she asked, her excitement undimmed by Carol's growing frustration.

Reaching her limit, Carol stood up abruptly, her movements quick and decisive. She marched over to Aditi, grabbed the clothes, and tossed them back onto the bed in a huff. With a steady grip, she steered Aditi towards the door, her voice firm and commanding. "Enough. Get going now. Just coffee and back. No dinner or drinks. Even if the guy asks."

In a twist of irony, Carol found herself spouting pragmatic wisdom, while Aditi, lost in the excitement of the meeting, seemed to have forsaken her customary prudence.

*

The atmosphere thickened with anticipation in the dimly lit corner of the reunion venue.

"Guys, now comes the sad part," Carol's voice broke the brief silence, heavy with emotion. "Do you really want to hear this? Why dampen the spirits today, at our reunion?" She glanced around, her eyes glistening with unshed tears.

"You've started it, so you might as well finish it. She was my friend too, you know." Ajay's effort to sound concerned barely concealed his nervousness, betraying his pressing need to understand the fallout from his previous actions.

Shehnaz, on the other hand, exhibited a softer approach, her empathy shining through. "No, Ajay. We should let it be if it's so painful for Carol."

Their gaze fell upon Carol, waiting for her decision.

After contemplating, she resolved to continue, "Hmmm...let me finish. And yes, Shehnaz, you can try to make sense of it as an experienced psychologist."

This acknowledgement of Shehnaz's professional background hinted at the complexity of the emotional landscape they were about to traverse.

Carol took a deep breath, steadying herself, "So she went to Vaishali to meet this cop guy."

22

Anticipation

The evening at Vaishali restaurant was like any other, bustling with the chatter of patrons, yet for Aditi, the world seemed to narrow down to the table she occupied in the sit-out area.

She arrived with a flutter in her stomach, a mix of anticipation and nervousness in how she continually adjusted her hair as she was escorted to her table.

Having dressed to impress, she found herself fidgeting, smoothing her outfit, rearranging her hair, trying to strike the perfect balance between casual and carefully put together.

It was an unusual sight. Aditi, always so composed, now seemed almost vulnerable, her eyes scanning the crowd for a face she had only seen in a photograph.

The minutes ticked by, turning into hours, and the empty coffee cups in front of her were a bitter reminder of the time spent waiting. The initial flush of excitement that had painted her cheeks rosy had long since faded, leaving her looking forlorn and increasingly agitated.

As the evening wore on, the once lively atmosphere of Vaishali began to dim, with the overhead lights casting long shadows across the tables. Aditi, still seated, appeared more isolated than ever, her hopeful glances at the entrance becoming fewer and further between.

The waiter's arrival to inquire if she wished to order anything more, seemed to snap her from her reverie. His question only added insult to injury. With a flash of irritation, she dismissed him, her anger not truly directed at him but at the situation, at the realisation that she had been stood up.

*

The atmosphere turned sombre as Carol continued to unveil the painful chapter from Aditi's past. Enveloped in uncomfortable silence, Ajay listened intently while Shehnaz, occasionally casting worried glances his way, appeared to be pondering the eventual outcome.

Carol's frustration showed as she recounted the heart-wrenching ordeal Aditi faced. "That guy never showed up! What a fucking jerk!" she exclaimed, her apology to Shehnaz for the harsh language barely masking her lingering anger.

Ajay and Shehnaz sat motionless, unsure how to react to the revelation.

"What did Aditi do?" Ajay found himself asking, despite the growing knot of apprehension in his stomach.

"What could she do?" Carol replied, her voice softening. "The poor girl waited three hours for him at Vaishali."

She continued, her voice heavy with disappointment, "She sent him a bunch of emails, seeking answers as to why he didn't appear. Unfortunately, the jerk never responded – not a single word."

Ajay's question, "So they never met?" resulted in an angry look from Shehnaz, annoyed by the pretence.

"But that wasn't all," Carol continued, her voice tinged with sadness. "For five days, Aditi showed up at Vaishali every evening, hoping he'd appear. She even had Babu on the lookout, asking him to inform her if a visitor from Mumbai inquired after her."

"Babu?" Shehnaz interjected, curious about this new character in their story.

"Yes, Babu from Mutha's Provision Store right beside Vaishali. He was our go-to for passing messages," Carol clarified. "Ajay, you remember him, right?"

Ajay gave a quiet nod, his mind seemingly elsewhere, not eager to dive back into those memories.

The mention of Aditi's unwavering hope painted a heartbreaking picture of the depth of her feelings.

Carol shared more about the misery that had enveloped Aditi, "That girl was devastated, in bad shape," Carol recounted. "I tried my best to console her and talk some sense into her, but to no avail. She felt utterly betrayed, deceived."

*

At Kamala Nehru Park, a deep sense of somberness filled the air.

Aditi and Carol found themselves on a secluded bench, Carol not able to gaze upon Aditi's tear-streaked face.

"Come on, Aditi. It's okay. He was not the right guy for you; I mean, you hadn't even met him," Carol attempted to soothe her friend, though her words felt hollow against the weight of Aditi's despair.

"Why did he have to do this to me? Why? Why?" Aditi sobbed, her voice breaking on each question.

"It's all for the best. Isn't it good that you found out now what a bastard he is, and not later?" Carol tried again to find a silver lining.

Yet, Aditi's tears refused to be stemmed, her sobs growing louder, echoing the depth of her pain. "He...he...seemed like such a decent chap. Why are men like this, Carol?" she cried out.

Carol put her arm around Aditi in a moment of shared sorrow, pulling her close in solidarity and comfort.

Aditi rested her head on Carol's shoulder, crying her heart out.

23

Into the Wee Hours

In the banquet hall, dimly lit and almost empty, staff members lingered nearby, their respectful presence a silent plea for the last three revellers to conclude their intense conversation so they could close up for the night.

Looking around, Carol turned to Ajay and Shehnaz. "Guys, this place is starting to feel a bit gloomy. Plus, the staff are waiting for us to leave."

Shehnaz quickly agreed, "Yes, we should probably head out. And Carol, it's too late for you to be going back alone. Let's call it a night."

Carol waved off the concern, "It's alright. I have my driver, and the city's still awake. But if you are both ready to leave, then sure."

Ajay, eager to hear the rest of the story, proposed an alternative: "How about we move to the coffee shop here? I bet it's still open. It will be a nice change of scenery. Maybe we could do another round of drinks?"

Shehnaz set a boundary, "Coffee sounds fine. But let's skip more alcohol."

Carol nodded in agreement, "A coffee, then we split."

Transitioning to the coffee shop, bustling with late-night patrons seeking a caffeine fix or a bite to sober up, the trio found themselves in a more upbeat setting.

"How's the Pune night scene now, Carol?" Ajay inquired, reflecting on their more constrained past. "We had limited options back then."

"Pune's buzzing these days, with all the new pubs, lounge bars, and eateries. Plus, the old favourites like Vaishali, Marzorin and Goodluck still thrive. Your 'limited options' were more from being perpetually broke," Carol laughed.

"That's because you girls always made us foot the bill for chaat, milkshakes and coffees at Vaishali," Ajay retorted.

"Never," Carol countered with a smile. "I don't recall a single instance of you boys paying. You probably squandered it all on cigarettes and booze."

She then told Shehnaz, "The hostel boys were notorious. So broke, they'd coax locals and fellow students to invite them for a meal at their homes. Afterwards, the place looked like they'd been through a battle."

"Why?" Shehnaz asked, intrigued.

"Are you going to tell her, or should I?" Carol teased Ajay, who wore a guilty grin.

"Huh? What? I don't know what you're talking about," he said, feigning innocence.

"They acted famished, like they hadn't eaten for days," Carol explained.

"Well, we were broke, and the hostel dining hall food was terrible," Ajay confessed, thinking back to their food fights with inedible fare. "We even protested the dreadful meals with thali-banging way before it became a thing during Covid!"

Shehnaz laughed, then asked, "So, what went down at these 'food parties' at friends' houses?"

Carol elaborated, "The same chaos. Fights over food, dish snatching and mad dashes with dishes through the house. It was a spectacle with the host's family present – parents, even grandparents, leaving them utterly traumatised. Naturally, there were no second invites."

"Seriously?" Shehnaz was astounded. "The boys sound a crazy lot. Savages."

"Totally," Carol concurred with a nod. "And let's not forget the stuff they'd nick just for the heck of it – ashtrays, spoons and forks from hotels. Tablecloths from events repurposed as bedsheets, curtains, and even *lungis*. And yes, even road signs – all hoarded as trophies in their rooms."

"Hope you didn't resort to taking things from the hosts' homes," Shehnaz asked Ajay, half-joking yet half-serious.

"It's quite possible," Carol responded with a mischievous glint in her eye.

"Enough of the ganging up," Ajay cut in, seeking a reprieve from the playful yet relentless teasing. "You hostel girls weren't exactly angels either. Trust me, you don't want me to get started!"

"Oh, really? Start on what? There's nothing you can say about us girls!" Carol retorted, throwing down the gauntlet.

Caught without an immediate comeback but unwilling to concede, Ajay grinned. "I can. I definitely can. Let's wait for tomorrow when Viru is there too," he said, buying time and keeping the banter light.

Their detour into a recall of hostel antics briefly lightened the mood, allowing them a momentary escape from the graver topic.

"So, you want me to finish the story?" Carol sighed, the grimness returning to the gathering.

Shehnaz and Ajay signalled their readiness to dive back into the narrative with subtle nods.

"I was just getting to how Aditi felt after being stood up at Vaishali that evening," Carol picked up the story again. "She was heartbroken, shattered, deeply affected," she said, her voice laced with sadness and empathy. "I attempted to console her and bring some perspective to the situation, but nothing helped. She felt profoundly betrayed and misled; she just could not get over it."

"Oh God! How long did this last?" Shehnaz inquired.

"Yes, when did she get over this?" Ajay added, hoping for a glimmer of redemption from Aditi's story.

Carol's response was a blow no one was prepared for. "Ajay, Shehnaz, that is the sad part. She never got over it! That incident scarred her, and she lost it," she revealed.

The sudden arrival of a few classmates, who had made a getaway to the Club's Irish pub and were now laden with "ones for the road," briefly halted the conversation. Their loud goodbyes as they staggered out starkly contrasted with the seriousness of their ongoing discussion.

"Stay safe, take a cab. Don't drive!" Carol called out after them.

Once they were alone again, Ajay, visibly shaken, stuttered, "Wh..at? Wh..at? What are...you...saying? Aditi has completely lost it?"

Carol, her frustration mounting, confirmed, "Yes, Ajay. She never recovered from that."

"But she went to Delhi for her Masters, right? She would have forgotten all this there," Ajay countered, clinging to hope.

Shehnaz, too, sought solace in the possibility of a new beginning for Aditi, "Yes, moving out of Pune would have helped her. University, studies, new place, and friends...?"

Carol's glare was a silent scream of Aditi's pain, her voice rising with each word, "You two don't get it! Aditi never left Pune, guys! She did not go to Delhi. Forget studies; she just gave up on everything!!"

"Oh! Where is she now? What does she do?" Ajay asked.

Carol's anger was palpable, her patience worn thin, "Haven't you been listening, Ajay? Aditi never left Pune! She is here in town! Always has been!"

Shehnaz intervened in a plea for calm, even as she inquired further, "What does Aditi do now, Carol?"

The answer laid bare the magnitude of Aditi's fall from the bright future she once had looked at. "It's disheartening – she never pursued a career! A brilliant girl like her. She takes English classes for little children in a primary school these days. It's been a constant struggle for her to make ends meet. I help her out with money sometimes," Carol shared, her voice heavy with sorrow.

Shehnaz's query about Aditi's personal life and marriage received a bleak response, "Marriage! She developed deep-rooted trust issues and said that she'd never look at another man. Moreover, her self-confidence plummeted. All because of that guy, whoever the hell he is!"

Carol's final revelation left a chilling silence in its wake. "She is in bad shape. I don't like to say this, but you are friends I trust," she confided, barely whispering. "She is dealing with alcohol issues, and is in and out of rehab centres."

The impact of Carol's words left Ajay and Shehnaz stunned.

"I make sure to visit her each time she is readmitted," Carol mentioned.

24

Anguish

The sombre ambience of the rehab centre's private room was undeniable as Carol sat across from an Aditi significantly altered by the years of addiction.

The impact showed in her appearance; her prematurely grey and unkempt hair framed a face marred by life's hardships, and her eyes were dull and unfocused.

Carol, despite the heaviness in her heart, greeted her friend cheerfully. "Hii, Aditi. How are you?"

But the response she received was far from the friendly banter of their college days. Aditi, agitated and barely containing her anger, immediately pressed, "Did you find him?"

Knowing fully well what Aditi meant, Carol still feigned ignorance. "Who?" she asked.

Aditi's frustration boiled over as she shouted, "You know who! Did you find him?"

The room fell silent for a moment, Carol's sorrow deepening as she gazed at her friend, whose mind was ensnared by an obsession with the man she had never met, this AK Louis. With a gentle squeeze of Aditi's hand, she attempted to anchor her back to reality. "Oh, Aditi, forget it. It was a long time back."

But Aditi's anguish was not to be soothed. "Even if you don't help me, I will find him! And kill him! Kill him!" she exclaimed.

*

Shehnaz and Ajay sat stunned, grappling with the gravity of Aditi's plight as Carol unveiled more layers of her condition.

The suffocating silence was broken only by Shehnaz's stuttered acknowledgement. "Oh…that is terrible."

Carol had more depressing news to share. "She's been having frequent meltdowns and becomes hysterical. Sometimes, she even threatens guys. And she's on medication."

The revelation hung heavily between them.

"Just a few days ago, I was in town for work and to check out this venue. Like I usually do, I stopped by her apartment, and that's when I saw one of these episodes firsthand."

*

The modest, somewhat shabby apartment was shrouded in the gloom of neglect.

The room, cluttered and dimly lit, bore witness to Aditi's descent into self-imposed solitary confinement. The telling presence of a half-empty whisky bottle underscored her surrender to desolation.

Sitting across from Aditi, Carol tried to pierce the dense fog that enveloped her once vibrant friend.

"How have you been, Aditi? Taking care of yourself, I hope?"

Aditi remained silent.

A persistent Carol offered a lifeline, "I am in town for a day. Want to have dinner out?"

Aditi's response was cold. "I am not interested. Why do you care? I never asked you to come."

Despite Aditi's rebuff, undeterred Carol continued, "Aditi, come on. I am your friend. You had gone silent, and I was worried."

"No one needs to worry about me. Leave!"

"Did you have lunch? I brought samosas and chocolate for dessert. Please, have something," Carol urged, trying to coax her friend into a semblance of normalcy.

"Stop worrying about me! I told you I'm okay!" Aditi's frustration boiled over.

"Alright," Carol conceded, a heavy silence settling between them as she searched for a safer subject.

"How are things at school? I hope all our CSR funds have been received. Are the kids having fun with the new iPads?" Carol ventured.

"Yeah, yeah, they are fine. Everyone is fine except me," Aditi snapped back.

Ignoring the tension, Carol smiled, desperate to lighten the mood. "You know, my niece, Sushma, the teenager you met in Mumbai a few years ago, is getting engaged. She's all grown up! And so excited."

But Aditi's reaction was so caustic that it visibly shocked Carol. "Who is she getting engaged to? Some spineless jerk who will abandon her?"

Flustered by her unsuccessful attempt to steer the conversation towards lighter topics, Carol felt her patience slipping.

"ADITI! Stop, for God's sake!" she exclaimed.

Aditi, however, was beyond consolation, her frustration tipping her over into a rant. "You should know better, Carol. Your husband left you. That bastard dumped me. Now, you want your niece to suffer, too? He will dump her!" she shouted, her voice laden with bitterness. "When will women learn? When?"

Carol's frustration turned to anger, stung by Aditi's attacks. "Aditi, my situation was different. I chose to end my marriage.

Please don't compare our circumstances. Don't project your anger onto others!"

Lost in the storm of her vendetta, Aditi shouted, "Shut up, Carol! I'll find him, and I'll kill him! I swear I will!"

Aditi's emotional collapse was sudden and total, her anger dissolving into sobs. Carol immediately moved to her side, enveloping her gently and reassuringly.

In a soft, caring tone, she comforted, "Aditi, it's okay, I'm here."

25

A Dark Place

Carol's voice cut through the sober mood in the now emptying coffee shop. "I thought of tracking down and confronting that jerk myself," her voice wavering between anger and sadness. "Aditi's life is ruined; she's in a dark place now."

Carol scrolled through her phone, showing them unsettling photos of Aditi's piercing gaze and dishevelled appearance, as well as a disturbing video of an angry outburst at the rehab centre.

"Did her parents not come and stay with her?" Shehnaz inquired, hoping for a sliver of hope in the bleak narrative.

"They tried but weren't able to be of any help. The cut has gone deep," Carol sighed.

Ajay remained silent in his turmoil, grappling with his secret and its unintended consequences.

As Carol pondered aloud the lasting impact of the deception, Shehnaz offered her professional insight. "Deceptive or humiliating incidents can cause lasting emotional harm. The extent varies based on the person's resilience."

Ajay, caught in his web of guilt, could hardly bear to listen.

"But Aditi was strong," Carol interjected, puzzling over the drastic change in her friend.

Shehnaz suggested, "People are complex. Such a person's self-esteem can take a hard hit after being jilted. It erodes self-image. But then, they may also seek validation from someone else and move on."

Yet, Aditi's story seemed far from a simple tale of moving on.

Shehnaz paused thoughtfully, then added, "Aditi's reaction might indicate deeper issues that may not have surfaced during your interactions in college. If someone already has underlying vulnerabilities, such as attachment issues or a history of emotional neglect, a traumatic event like being jilted can amplify those weaknesses. They may struggle with feelings of worthlessness or develop unhealthy coping mechanisms. This isn't just about being weak-willed; it's about how past experiences shape our responses to new traumas."

Carol nodded slowly, considering Shehnaz's insight. She said, "Yes, I can see where you're going with this. It's very nuanced. So, you're saying there could have been a dimension to Aditi's personality that she suppressed during college, right?"

"Yes," replied Shehnaz. "It's one possibility. Maybe not consciously suppressed, just that no triggers brought it to the fore."

Carol responded with a "Hmm" as she quietly reflected on it. She soon offered her bit of analysis. "I'm beginning to think Aditi's steering clear of romantic involvements in college stemmed from deeper conflict. Maybe childhood trauma. We all thought it was Aditi being Aditi – fiercely independent and idealistic."

Amused by Carol's newfound expertise and insights, Shehnaz thought, *I guess I wasted all those years studying psychology. I could have just hung out with a few experts at parties and become one myself.*

Keen to end the pointless analysis, Shehnaz surmised, "Whether Aditi's behaviour, though typical of the reaction of a weak-willed individual, stems from past trauma isn't something we can pass judgement on now. There's no point speculating."

She gently suggested, "Carol, you have been a true friend and stood by Aditi through her difficult times. Encourage her to seek professional help. Pune has some great doctors. I can refer a couple."

Carol nodded in agreement. "Thanks, Shehnaz. I'd appreciate that."

She then announced that she had sent Aditi a copy of Ajay's new book, hoping it might lift her spirits. Ajay's reaction, a mix of worry and fear, did not go unnoticed by Shehnaz.

As they prepared to leave, Carol mentioned their plan to visit Fergusson College the next day. Ajay and Shehnaz, still sombre, agreed quietly.

Exiting into the lobby, Carol apologised for the evening's gloomy turn. "Sorry, I must have spooked you with that story. Maybe I shouldn't have given you so much detail."

"It's okay, Carol," said Shehnaz, offering reassurance as Ajay silently walked beside them.

But the evening's revelations hung heavily between them.

26

The Aftermath

The ride back to the hotel was shrouded in a thick veil of silence, starkly contrasting the light-hearted banter and anticipation they had felt on their way to the reunion.

Shehnaz finally broke the silence, her voice laced with disappointment and disbelief.

"See what your stupid prank in college did to her," she said, trying to keep her voice even.

Lost in his turmoil, Ajay offered no response, his gaze fixed on the passing city lights.

Shehnaz's frustration mounted as she addressed him again, more forcefully this time, "Ajay! I am talking to you." He turned to face her, his expression a mixture of guilt and defensiveness.

"What do you want me to say? How the hell was I to know that this would be the consequence!" he retorted, his voice rising in frustration.

Shehnaz, unwavering, pressed on. "Ajay, reach out to her, meet her and apologise. It's the only way she will find closure and move on."

Ajay refused immediately, his voice tinged with anger, "I didn't ask for your professional advice. No, I can't meet her. You don't think I regret it? I feel terrible. Don't make it worse, Shehnaz. Why do you care? You don't even know Aditi!"

The intensity of their exchange caught the driver's attention, prompting him to look at them through the rear-view mirror.

"Shinde, get us to the hotel quickly. What's taking so long?" Ajay barked.

The hotel room at JW Mariott was wrapped in silence, the air thick with the unresolved tension between Ajay and Shehnaz.

In the dim light, they each faced away from the other in bed. Ajay turned off the lamp with a flick, casting the room into darkness.

Restlessness gripped Ajay as he lay awake, Carol's stories of Aditi's struggles replaying in his mind. Eventually, sleep claimed him but offered no escape.

Soon, Ajay found himself trapped in a nightmare, a vivid reenactment of Carol's narrative where the haunting image of Aditi from Carol's phone transformed into a presence looming ominously at the foot of their bed.

A strangled scream tore through the silence of the room, jolting Shehnaz awake. Confused and concerned, she turned to Ajay, whose eyes were fixed on a spot where he imagined the ghostly figure of Aditi stood.

"What is it, Ajay?" asked Shehnaz.

Turning on the light, she scanned the room, finding nothing amiss. Still gripped by the remnants of his nightmare, Ajay hesitated, then frantically checked the room.

"You scared me! Did you have a nightmare?" Shehnaz's tone softened as she figured out the cause of Ajay's distress.

Ajay, still caught in the after-effects of his dream, remained silent.

"Go back to sleep," Shehnaz urged gently, reaching for the light switch again.

"No, keep the night light on," Ajay's voice was a mere whisper, a plea for some semblance of security against the shadows that lingered in his mind.

In the tranquil morning ambience of the hotel's spacious dining hall, Ajay and Shehnaz were enveloped in profound silence punctuated by the occasional clink of cutlery.

The usually comforting aroma of brewing coffee and freshly baked bread failed to break the impasse at their table. Ajay cradled a cup of coffee, lost in the haunting details about Aditi disclosed by Carol the night before. Meanwhile, Shehnaz, having enjoyed a lavish breakfast, sought to draw Ajay out of his pensive state.

Observing Ajay's neglected meal, Shehnaz gently prodded, "Aren't you going to eat, Ajay?"

"I don't feel like it. I didn't sleep well; I had a terrible night," Ajay admitted, fatigue evident in his voice.

"Been thinking about the Aditi issue?" Shehnaz probed.

Ajay remained silent, and the lack of response confirmed her suspicions.

Shehnaz, seeking to offer some comfort, said, "Forget it. There's not much you or anyone can do. It's unfortunate."

Ajay could only muster a noncommittal "Mmm."

While Shehnaz took in Ajay's visible distress, searching for a resolution, his phone rang.

"Hi, Carol," Ajay answered.

"Hey Ajay, I hope you are on your way to college. I will be there in ten minutes," said Carol energetically. She was determined to gather the old friends at Fergusson College, an integral part of their reunion agenda.

Caught off-guard, Ajay said, "No, Carol, we are at breakfast; we are running late," hinting at a reluctance to participate in the day's plans.

Carol prodded, "You okay, Ajay? You don't sound good."

"Just tired. Honestly, Carol, I'm not in the mood to come to college," Ajay said, hesitating to visit the place teeming with memories now tainted by the recent revelations.

Carol continued, "No, Ajay! You can't say that. It is part of the reunion plan. You have to come!"

Ajay, seeking Shehnaz's opinion, was caught in a tug-of-war between his apprehensions and Carol's persistence.

"Carol. She is going to Fergusson and wants us to come. She's insisting," he relayed to Shehnaz.

Shehnaz left the decision in his hands: "It's up to you. Either way is fine for me."

After pausing momentarily, Ajay remained non-committal, unsure how to wriggle out. "Carol. I'm not sure."

Carol responded with annoyance, "*Don't do this to me, Ajay*! I have called Viru and Prakash. God knows when we will all meet next. Come on, Ajay."

The finality in her voice left little room for further discussion, leading Ajay to yield. "Okay, okay, Carol. We will be there. We will leave here in about twenty minutes."

Satisfied with the outcome, Carol didn't forget to remind him, "Great, Ajay. And Shehnaz, too, right?"

With the phone call concluded, Ajay turned to Shehnaz. "Let's get this done with. Let's leave as soon as you finish."

What was intended to be an enjoyable walk down memory lane now looked like an unpleasant chore.

27

Hanuman Tekdi

As the morning sun cast a golden hue over Fergusson College, Ajay, Shehnaz, Carol and Viru walked into the historic college, where the past intertwined with the present.

The sprawling campus, known for its blend of Gothic and Indian architectural styles, stood as a testament to Fergusson College's rich heritage and academic excellence.

Viru gazed fondly at a familiar spot in front of the Main Building and remarked, "There is our *khatta*, where we used to unwind between classes," evoking a shared nostalgia among the group.

With a reflective smile, Carol added, "Those were some of the best years of my life. The memories and friendships we made here are unforgettable."

The majestic main building of Fergusson College, designed during the British Raj, had Ajay proudly showing Shehnaz over the campus.

Shehnaz, impressed, commented, "Fergusson College has a remarkable history."

This prompted Carol to add, "Exactly, and it boasts notable alumni like former Prime Ministers VP Singh and Narasimha Rao."

"Any other notable figures?" Shehnaz inquired, "Apart from this famous group, of course."

Viru, perhaps surprisingly to some given his laidback college persona, contributed, "Yes, the college has strong ties to Indian politics, going back to the Independence movement and the Indian National Congress. Bal Gangadhar Tilak was one of the founders of this college back in 1885. Veer Savarkar studied here. His room in the hostel is preserved as a memorial."

Carol playfully ribbed, "*Wah*, Viru. You didn't know where the classrooms were back then, and now you're a walking history book!"

This was met with Viru's good-natured grin. "I am with the government's Education Department. I had better know something!"

The conversation then turned to Fergusson College's Bollywood connections, with Carol listing alumni such as Sai Paranjpye, Dr. Sriram Lagoo, Smita Patil and others. "The Film and Television Institute – FTII is next door. And some scenes from Richard Attenborough's *Gandhi* were shot on campus, in the Gymkhana grounds and amphitheatre," she added, underscoring the college's association with film and the arts.

Ajay, ever the adventurer, proposed, "Enough, history buffs! Who's up for a climb up Hanuman Tekdi?"

At Shehnaz's inquiry about the Tekdi, Ajay explained, "It's the hill behind the campus. I think we also used to refer to it as Fergusson Hill. There is a Hanuman temple at the top. Sometimes, we would jog up there in the mornings and stargaze at night."

"Stargazing? Is that what you wanted everyone to believe you were doing?" Carol interjected with a smirk. "I've heard that the hostel boys would venture up there after dark, hoping to sneak a peek at the girls from Sophia's campus on the opposite side. Talk about desperation!"

"That's just rumours," Viru retorted in defence. "Besides, what does that say about the girls at Fergusson?"

"Great comeback, Viru," Ajay applauded with a laugh. "Seriously, though, that hike up the hill... anyone up for it?"

His challenge was met with little enthusiasm. Carol opted out. "Nah, I just want to soak in the campus, walk around, and revisit old spots. *Chalo.*"

They meandered through the college, admiring the intricate details of the stone buildings that adorned the campus. Each structure, made from locally sourced stone, told a story of a time when Fergusson College was at the forefront of education and the freedom struggle.

Walking past the majestic NM Wadia Amphitheatre, an embodiment of semi-Gothic architectural splendour dating back to 1912, one was transported through over a century of history.

The contributions from a prominent Parsi benefactor and Prince Aga Khan to the amphitheatre's construction underscored an early recognition that unity among diverse groups was essential to lay the groundwork for propagating the ideals of an independent India.

This three-level edifice echoed the spirited discussions and debates of luminaries from the Indian Freedom Movement, politics and literature. Personalities such as Rabindranath Tagore, Sarojini Naidu, Jawaharlal Nehru, VD Savarkar and Sarvepalli Radhakrishnan, along with many others, initiated movements, inspired minds and driven action with their passionate pleas and speeches.

It stood as a beacon of the freedom of debate and the assimilation of diverse and often contrasting viewpoints. The amphitheatre continued to nurture these ideals, serving as a platform where contemporary thinkers and policymakers engaged with students, sparking debates and fostering introspection.

The group converged before the Bai Jerbai Wadia Library, an emblem of knowledge and heritage. Constructed in 1929, it was a highlight of the campus with its over two hundred thousand books collection.

"I bet we walked past the library and amphitheatre thousands of times heading to and from the canteen, and I can't recall ever actually going inside or even really looking at them," Carol mused.

"Funny, isn't it? Back then, they were just stone buildings! It took us twenty-five years to appreciate their significance and grandeur," Ajay reflected.

"Pity. Maybe we should propose to the college that they include a heritage walk for all new students during orientation," Carol proposed. "To fully appreciate and value the esteemed institution they belong to."

The morning had been heavy with nostalgia, which Viru found a tad overwhelming. His suggestion to head to the canteen, with its allure of bun wada sambar and chai, subtly shifted the group's focus from history to their favourite haunt.

"*Chalo* canteen! Lead the way, Viru!" Carol exclaimed as they headed towards the iconic spot.

28

High Noon at Fergusson

"This town ain't big enough for both of us."

Ajay, who was walking briskly ahead of the group, suddenly stopped, spun around to face Viru, and delivered the line with dramatic flair.

Ajay had been deeply distressed by Carol's revelation at the reunion party and had wanted to skip the college walk-through. However, the gloomy memories of the previous evening faded once there. His long-held desire to show Shehnaz this cherished fragment of his life took over, and he became excited and upbeat. Fergusson and Pune would always be close to his heart, lifting his spirits like the comforting familiarity of canteen chai.

"This town ain't big enough for both of us, pardner," Ajay repeated.

The rest of the group gave him quizzical looks, and Viru asked, "*Yeda hai kya*? What are you blabbering about?"

"*When you have to shoot, shoot. Don't talk,*" Ajay fired off another line from a Western.

"Are you okay, Ajay?" Carol asked, her voice laced with mock concern before she added with a smirk, "You're delirious. The heat must have gotten to you. We'd better head indoors soon."

"Guys, what does this place remind you of?" Ajay responded, gesturing broadly with his arm. "Just look around."

They had walked in the blazing sun on dusty pathways, between the stone buildings and isolated outhouses amidst an arid landscape with a hill in the backdrop. The amphitheatre and library, tall, arched structures resembling courthouses and churches, evoked the feel of a frontier town, a setting straight out of an old Western.

Closed windows set in imposing stone walls and a scattering of students hurrying by signalled that the appointed hour for a duel was nearing. The scene was nearly perfect; the only elements missing were the sounds of hooves and the haunting whistling score from *The Good, the Bad, and the Ugly*.

"Aren't you getting the vibes? This is straight out of a Louis L'Amour book," Ajay explained.

"Louis? Louis, who?" Carol asked, puzzled.

"Louis L'Amour, the author of Western novels. Haven't you heard of him? Louis L'Amour," Ajay reiterated, hoping to clarify. Then he added sarcastically, "What about Clint Eastwood? Heard of him?"

"Of course," Carol responded. Looking around, she added, "I don't see any connection between all that and the college."

Ajay replied with resignation, "Forget it. It's wasted on you guys. Anyway, Carol, you were into Mills and Boon back then. And Viru, you never read anything – except for those glossy magazines you kept hidden under the mattress."

"National Geographic," Viru clarified to the rest, eager to dispel any misconceptions.

"Yeah, they were graphic alright!" Ajay shot back.

The girls, eager to escape the heat and get indoors, quickly moved past the boys and the topics only they seemed to connect with.

As Fergusson College's canteen came into view around the next turn, a wave of nostalgia washed over the group, leaving them transfixed.

The scene was deeply familiar, mirroring the countless times they had entered during their three years at college. It felt as though their twenty-year-old selves were about to step into the canteen after a series of gruelling lectures.

The canteen, with its modest tiled roof, was nestled under the canopy of two trees that flanked it. The entire front was marked by a vibrant but incongruous blue grill sitting atop a three-foot tall blue wall. The open metallic doors, painted blue with a grill and metal bottom, matched the walls. The dim interiors contrasted with the bright sunlight outside, creating a veil of darkness. The open doors were the only indication that the canteen was open for business.

Advertising banners for soft drinks added a contemporary touch to the otherwise traditional structure. In front of the canteen, the dusty, unpaved ground and roughly placed slabs leading to the steps contributed to the rustic charm. This created a relaxed, almost nostalgic atmosphere, a popular gathering spot for students to stand and sip chai when the canteen was too full or stifling.

"Wow, can you believe this place hasn't changed a bit?" Ajay exclaimed. "Look at that! It's like stepping into a time machine!"

Shehnaz, less impressed by the canteen's exterior, raised an eyebrow. "This is the famous canteen you've been talking about? This looks...rundown."

Ajay laughed, scanning the familiar surroundings. "It's not about how it looks, Shehnaz. It's about the memories. This place was our second home."

Carol nodded in agreement, a soft smile playing on her lips. "Exactly. It's the memories that count. I'm glad some things stay the same. There's a newer second canteen on campus, but this one is ours!"

Together, they walked inside, their steps echoing in the semi-empty space. The sounds of sizzling batata wadas and the aroma of chai instantly transported them back to their college days. The mismatched furniture and peeling posters only added to the charm, each an element of their shared history.

Finding their way to their old haunt, a corner table that had witnessed endless debates, laughter, and the occasional heart-to-heart, they settled in. The wooden chairs and tables bore the marks and scratches of frequent use, some probably dating back a couple of decades.

Looking around, Viru remarked, "The canteen was much brighter and airier back then."

The walls of the canteen were covered with large, colourful billboards advertising soft drinks, occupying significant wall space and reducing the inflow of natural light through the grilled back of the canteen, which offered glimpses of the Gymkhana grounds and Hanuman Tekdi.

The waiter, recognising the look in their eyes, approached with a knowing smile as if welcoming back old friends.

"Let's order some bun wada sambar and chai," Viru suggested, his eyes sparkling with anticipation. "Just like old times."

"And omelette, and cream rolls, and upeet and sheera," Ajay added excitedly, eager to savour the fare he had been craving since the reunion was announced.

As they placed their order, the canteen's ambient noise faded into the background, replaced by their excited chatter. The group was momentarily transported back to a time when life was simpler.

Shehnaz found herself visualising the tales of campus life Ajay had shared with her. "So, this is the legendary canteen," Shehnaz mused, her plate heaped with the canteen's specialities, her voice mingling with the group's laughter.

"Yes, and it hasn't changed a bit," Ajay replied. "Hey, Viru, remember our hostel block? Fancy a trip to Block Four later to check out our old rooms?" To the rest, he proudly recounted, "The bunch of us had the last five rooms in the wing. Isolated and off-limits for everyone else!"

Viru, caught in the middle of a failed attempt at the old matchbox game, chuckled. "Sure, why not? Let's go later to the hostel. I see some new structures around." Reaching for Ajay's plate, he added, "Are you going to finish that bun wada?"

The college's incremental growth over the years, marked by the introduction of postgraduate programmes, diploma courses, and research centres, and a corresponding rise in student enrollment, had necessitated the erection of new buildings on the grounds, detracting from the predominantly stone structures that characterised the campus during the group's stay at Fergusson.

Soon enough, the boys became engrossed in the matchbox and glass game and failed spectacularly. Watching them, Carol chuckled and commented, "Boys will be boys!"

A group of young college students observed in amusement the youthful exuberance displayed by the fiftysomething-year-olds.

Shehnaz, who had patiently listened to their stories and moments over the last two days, glanced around the canteen. The nostalgia-laden chatter and inside jokes had initially amused her, but now she felt a bit bored. Watching the boys engrossed in their juvenile game, she couldn't help but feel even more alienated.

She sipped her drink, her mind wandering as the conversation continued without her.

It was then that Carol's sudden exclamation pierced the air.

"Oh my God!" Her voice, sharp and alarmed, instantly drew everyone's attention.

"What's wrong, Carol?" Viru asked as he followed Carol's fixed gaze across the canteen.

Without a word, Carol pointed towards the room's far end, her finger trembling slightly. "Look over there. At the back. The corner," she whispered, her voice heavy with disbelief. "Aditi!" she breathed.

As they turned their heads in unison, the laughter died in their throats.

In the shadows of the canteen, a solitary figure sat, both part of the scene and starkly isolated from it.

The dishevelled appearance, the hauntingly familiar eyes – yes, it was Aditi, unmistakably. Her gaze, intensified by the dramatic outline of kohl, cut sharply through the room.

As they reluctantly turned their gaze away from Aditi, Shehnaz felt a pang of empathy for the friend she'd never met.

29

Silver in the Dust

The unexpected sighting of Aditi in the canteen left the group in shock and disbelief. Viru, not privy to the previous night's revelations, couldn't seem to wrap his head around the reality of the situation. "Aditi? Our Aditi Joshi? Can't be!" he exclaimed.

"Yes, it is her," Carol confirmed.

As Aditi's gaze remained fixed on an unseen point in the distance, Viru, moved by a mix of concern and curiosity, offered, "Shall I go and talk to her? Is she unwell?"

"Ssshhh, Viru. Don't go there. It's a long story. Not now. Just sit here," Carol cautioned.

Amid their hushed conversation, they cast occasional nervous glances toward Aditi, who appeared absorbed in her thoughts, seemingly oblivious to the world around her.

Ajay, unsettled by the sight of Aditi, turned to Carol. "Carol! What is she doing here?"

Carol's response did little to alleviate the growing tension. "I don't know, Ajay. She never meets classmates or comes to college. Like I told you, her mental state is very fragile."

Viru's confusion turned to distress, "What? Mental state? What are you saying, Carol?"

Carol's patience was wearing thin, "Viru, will you please shut up for a minute? I'll tell you later."

The tension escalated when Aditi began flipping through the pages of a book she had picked up from her table.

The title *Reflections* was visible, causing Ajay's face to pale noticeably.

Carol's inquiry, "That book, Ajay, is it yours? The short stories book," only deepened his unrest.

Ajay's face drained of colour as he muttered in distress. "Oh no! No. No. The book. The story."

Carol and Viru looked at him, puzzled.

Carol pressed him for an explanation, "What is it, Ajay? What about the book? What story?"

Ajay was becoming increasingly agitated, and his only thought was to escape, "Shehnaz, I think we should leave."

Before anyone could react, Aditi noticed their group and stood up. Her gaze was fixed on them as she picked up the book and slowly approached them.

Aditi's approach was deliberate and menacing, and her intense glare made everyone uncomfortable.

Ajay's voice quivered as Aditi advanced towards their table, "She is heading here! Shehnaz!"

Clutching the book *Reflections* tightly, Aditi approached them with a slow, deliberate stride. Her glare was fixed unflinchingly on Ajay, who appeared frozen.

Upon reaching the table, Aditi stood silently, her eyes burning with an intensity that seemed to pierce through Ajay.

Carol, eager to maintain a semblance of normality and avoid triggering Aditi, greeted her gingerly. "Hi, Aditi. It's good to see you." But Aditi's attention was solely on Ajay, her gaze unwavering and filled with an unspoken accusation.

Attempting introductions, Carol said, "Aditi, this is Viru. This is Ajay. From our gang, remember?"

Aditi's focus didn't waver from Ajay. Her question was direct and filled with an undercurrent of anger. "Why did you come?"

Carol tried to explain, mentioning the reunion and how Aditi had declined to attend, but Aditi was not interested in any of that. Instead, she held up Ajay's book, pointing to it. "You wrote this?" she asked.

"Yes...yes," Ajay confirmed.

"So then, you are the author of this story, *Silver in the Dust?*" she demanded.

"Aditi...I can explain," Ajay began, but before he could continue, Aditi slammed the book down on the table, causing the others to recoil.

"Answer my question, dammit!" she shouted.

"Yes," Ajay managed to utter.

"Yes, what? Yes, what?" Aditi pressed him further.

In a rush, Ajay stammered, "Yes...Yes, I...wrote that story."

"What is your name?" Aditi asked coldly.

A puzzled Carol tried to intervene, "Aditi, what is this? Why are you asking him all this? Why don't you sit down?"

Aditi, however, paid no heed to Carol and persisted, "What is your name?"

"Ajay," he replied.

"Hah. Ajay? Really? Did Ajay write that story? Or did someone else write it? Twenty-five years ago?" Aditi challenged.

Ajay fell silent, unable to respond, as Carol attempted once more to de-escalate the situation, "Aditi, please. Come, let's step outside. Let me take you home. Have you been taking your meds?"

"Shut the fuck up, Carol!" Aditi snapped. Carol recoiled in shock and fear at her dear friend's maniacal rage.

Aditi's focus was unwavering as she turned back to Ajay. "Tell me, who wrote this story?"

Again, Ajay offered no answer. Aditi, frustration mounting, banged her fist on the table.

Observing the unfolding drama, Shehnaz became distressed, "Ajay, we must leave. Let's go. This woman is scaring me," she said, her concern for their safety growing with each tense exchange.

Despite his fear, Ajay couldn't help but wonder why Shehnaz's professionalism had slipped. As a psychologist, she usually remained calm and collected in such situations. He glanced at her, noticing the uncharacteristic anxiety in her eyes. *Isn't this the kind of thing you deal with all the time? You should be the one diffusing it*, he thought, puzzled by her reaction.

"Shehnaz, it's okay," he said, trying to steady his nerves as he saw his wife sensing a threat and in distress. "Yes, let's leave."

Aditi whipped her head around with a sudden, sharp movement, fixing Shehnaz with a glare so intense it was as if she were under some maniacal spell.

The tension in the canteen ratcheted up as Aditi's focus narrowed onto Shehnaz. "Who is she? Who the fuck are you? Tell me!" Aditi's demanded.

The strong language caught the attention of a few canteen customers, who turned their heads in their direction.

Everyone at the table froze, their eyes wide with shock. Carol's hand flew to her mouth, stifling a gasp. Viru, usually the first to jump into action, hesitated, caught off-guard by the intensity of Aditi's outburst. There was a clear concern for Shehnaz, an outsider to their college group. Despite their shock, the friends felt a collective urge to buffer her from Aditi's unpredictable wrath.

"Who the fuck are you?" Aditi again asked aggressively.

Ajay, attempting to shield his wife, gently countered the maniacal Aditi, "Take it easy. This is my wife..."

But Aditi was unappeased. Her voice dripped with sarcasm as she mocked, "Wife. Aaah. The author has a wife." Aditi leaned in closer to Shehnaz, her finger tracing Shehnaz's cheek, a violation that sent shivers down Shehnaz's spine.

Aditi's taunts grew crueller, "You have done well for yourself, lover boy," she sneered at Ajay before turning her venomous attention back to Shehnaz. "What did you say? That I am scaring you? Scaring you, eh? You don't know the meaning of scared, sweetheart! You have not been to the dark places I have been! I can send you there."

Carol, shocked by Aditi's intensity, exclaimed, "Aditi! What are you saying? Why are you talking to them like that? Stop it!"

Carol's attempts to intervene fell on deaf ears. Aditi was beyond reach, caught up in a whirlwind of anger and despair. "Wife? Are you happily married? I am sure you two are a lovey-dovey couple," Aditi mocked, her words laced with bitterness and envy.

Aditi's relentless interrogation of Shehnaz then continued. "What's your name? What do you do?"

Shehnaz, visibly shaken, responded, "Shehnaz...I am... I am...a psychologist."

"Shehnaz, eh? A psychologist? My, my. Sexy Shehnaz is a psychologist!" Aditi added with an evil cackle, "Just what the doctor ordered!"

Suddenly, Aditi's demeanour softened as if a switch had been flipped.

"Oh, Shehnaz, don't be scared, sweetheart. You know something? I just wanted to live your life. Marriage. Career. Children. Happiness. Isn't that what every woman desires?"

But the moment of vulnerability was fleeting.

Aditi's voice rose again. "But what do I have instead? Nothing? A drab, boring existence. No love, no life. Trapped in the dust."

Her fury now squarely aimed at Ajay, Aditi accused, "Is that why you named your story *Silver in the Dust?* A mockery of me? I'm nothing but dust, right?"

Her glare was unyielding as she yelled. "All because of you! Ajay Rawal, the charming AK Louis!"

Carol's face was a mask of disbelief and horror as Aditi's words unraveled a secret that had remained hidden for a quarter of a century.

She looked around the canteen, where all activity had come to a standstill.

Minor scuffles between students in the canteen were not uncommon. However, it was pretty bizarre to see a group of middle-aged alumni engaging in what appeared to be a showdown. Students there were amused and somewhat intrigued, speculating that it might involve a love triangle. Some eagerly anticipated the dramatic conclusion of this *pati, patni aur woh* soap opera confrontation!

The all-male canteen staff stood around, exchanging glances, unsure how to handle the rapidly escalating situation involving a hostile female customer. The manager, perched on a stool behind the counter, turned down the canteen radio, eager to catch the drama unfolding before his eyes, even as he counted a wad of currency notes.

Carol, confounded by the unexpected turn of events and uncertain of the best course of action, decided to use reason.

"Aditi! How can you blame Ajay for your situation?" Carol interjected, trying to dial down the escalating situation. But Aditi was past reasoning, her fury undiminished as she accused Ajay with unrestrained anger.

"Carol! You don't know shit! Ajay is that guy: AK Louis. The one who never showed up in Vaishali twenty-five years ago! He destroyed my life! Tell her, you coward! Tell her!"

Carol's confusion morphed into shock, her voice barely a whisper as she tried to grasp the enormity of the revelation. "Ajay? AK Louis? The same guy?"

Aditi's confirmation cut deep, "There was no AK Louis. It was Ajay. He pretended to be the writer, AK Louis! Bastard!" Her words left Carol reeling, the pieces of a long-hidden puzzle falling into place most horrifyingly.

Carol's reaction was visceral. Her hand covered her mouth as she looked between Ajay and Aditi, searching for signs of a misunderstanding. But Ajay's silence spoke volumes, his guilt apparent in his inability to meet Carol's eyes.

"What is this, Ajay? Tell me, is it true?" Carol pleaded.

Then, as the truth dawned on her, anger took hold. "Oh God! I can't believe this! You are that guy? You sat and listened to Aditi's story at the party last night and did not say a word. I feel like an idiot. Ajay, you shit! Why did you do this to her?"

Carol's empathy for Aditi showed clearly, her voice cracking with emotion. "Oh, Aditi. Our friend did this to you. You poor girl."

Aditi's gaze remained locked on Ajay. "I've lost twenty-five years of my life because of you. I can never get them back," she stated.

Aditi's next words hung in the air, ominous and heavy with implication. "But you know what I can do?"

The question was a threat, a promise of retribution for the years of pain and loss.

"You know what I can do?" Aditi repeated.

Ajay's fear was unmistakable, his voice barely a whisper, "Wh..at? Wh..at?" as he realised the gravity of the situation.

Her words, spoken with a chilling calmness, detailed her twisted form of retribution. "So let's do the math. You have another twenty-five years of active life. Twenty-five years you, your pretty wife and your kids can enjoy. Holidays, kids' marriages, grandchildren, and friends. Twenty-five years of fun. Before age catches up."

The group is frozen, each member processing the horrifying logic of Aditi's revenge.

"I am going to take those twenty-five years away from you and your family. That's only fair, don't you think? I lost twenty-five years of my life because of you," Aditi continued, her voice rising with every word, her anger transforming into something dark and unfathomable.

Ajay's panic escalated. His movements became erratic as he accidentally knocked over a glass of water, and his voice trembled with fear. "What...do you mean?"

An evil smirk distorted Aditi's face as she suddenly screamed, "I am going to finish you, Ajay, so you don't get to enjoy those twenty-five years!"

Her arm shot up in a heartbeat, a fork clenched tightly in her hand, her target clear.

The gleaming metal was raised high; Aditi was poised to strike Ajay.

PART 3

Retribution

A Month Earlier

30

Globetrotter

The sun had begun its descent, casting elongated shadows across the shiny office towers of Bandra Kurla Complex – BKC – Mumbai's upscale business and residential district. Streetlights flickered to life as cabs lined the streets, anticipating the end of the workday and long-distance fares.

Located strategically between two of Mumbai's main north-south arteries, the Western Express Highway and the Eastern Express Highway, BKC was home to many corporate head offices, entertainment and shopping hubs, fine dining establishments, chic eateries and pubs.

The offices of ArrowHead Media, the new age, AI-based visual content creation platform, were housed on two floors of Pixel Towers, within range of many of its corporate customers, partners and bankers.

ArrowHead Media's founder and largest stakeholder, Carol D'Souza, sat in her spacious, well-appointed office on the fifth floor, surrounded by the symbols of her success. The soft hum of the day winding down filled the room as Smita, Carol's diligent secretary, popped her head in, signalling the close of another productive day.

"I am leaving for the day, ma'am. Is there anything you need before I go?" Smita asked.

Sitting back in her chair, Carol shook her head with a smile. "Thanks, Smita. No. You have a great evening. See you tomorrow," she replied. Carol was done for the day, having just concluded a marathon four-hour session with a bunch of investment bankers who were keen to manage her upcoming IPO.

As Smita left, Carol's demeanour shifted from an astute serial entrepreneur to someone caught in nostalgia. She picked up her phone, dialled a number, and waited for the call to connect.

"Hello," came Ajay's voice on the other end.

"Is this Ajay Rawal?" Carol asked, her voice tinged with excitement.

"Yes, who is calling?" Ajay responded.

"Guess!" Carol teased.

Ajay was taken aback. "Huh? Who is this?"

"Take a guess, yaar?" Carol insisted.

The conversation continued, and reminiscences and plans for an upcoming reunion weaved through their exchange. As the call drew to a close, Carol reminded Ajay of a small matter. "Okay, bye, Ajay. Don't forget to send me the Amazon link to your book."

Carol hung up, thought for a few seconds, and then dialled another number.

In the subdued light of New Delhi airport's VIP lounge, against the backdrop of ceaseless departures and arrivals, a passenger clad impeccably in business attire was absorbed in her laptop. The screen's glow cast a soft light on her refined features, with her flowing black hair complementing an expression of intense concentration. She relished a brief pause, enjoying a sip of coffee from an elegant china cup. Two uniformed security personnel stood at a distance, vigilantly keeping watch.

The seasoned diplomat, well-versed in the demands of international travel and critical negotiations, momentarily paused to address an official beside her. The mid-level bureaucrat, poised and ready to assist, presented a document to her. With a swift glance, she reviewed it, signed with a practised hand, and returned it, all within moments, resuming her work with unwavering focus.

Just then, her phone rang. She briefly glanced at the screen and looked up at the official. Dismissed by her unspoken cue, he quietly receded into the shadows.

Carol, still energised from her chat with Ajay, was excited about making the upcoming reunion unforgettable. She waited patiently for her call to be answered. "Hey. Finally. I have been trying to reach you for a couple of days. The phone was switched off. Calls were not returned!!"

Aditi, momentarily distracted from her work, apologised, her voice a blend of fatigue and warmth. "Sorry, Carol. Travel's been hectic. I am at the airport. Returning to London from a short trip. I would have called you," she explained.

"Yeah, hot-shot diplomat. Okay, I called about the reunion on 25 August. I told you earlier about it," Carol began.

Aditi responded with her usual grace under pressure. "I remember. The 25th of August is a bit of a challenge, Carol. I'll likely be back in Delhi holding meetings with the Ministry of External Affairs on G20-related matters. I'll breathe easier when India's G20 Presidency ends. The pressure is immense."

Carol suggested an alternative. "What about the 26th? We are meeting at Fergusson College. You can meet some of them, at least, if you come."

"That's possible, I think, if I take a late-night or early-morning flight out of Delhi," Aditi considered, finding a sliver of a gap in her hectic schedule.

Carol's voice brightened at the possibility. "That would be perfect. It's been ages since we all got together. And honestly, it would be lovely to have you join in, even if it's just for a day or two."

Carol then made an emotional appeal. "Aditi, please come to Pune. You know, we haven't really met after college. There's lots to catch up on. Do come, please."

"Carol, I, too want to meet and catch up with you. I will definitely try to make it," Aditi promised.

Their conversation drifted to updates and mutual acquaintances, with Carol sharing, "Oh, and I just spoke to Ajay Rawal. He's coming to the reunion, too."

Aditi asked, mildly curious, "Ajay? What's he up to these days? I've lost touch with most from our batch."

Carol chuckled, "He's doing quite well for himself. Can you believe he's now the CEO of a lifestyle company? And he's published a book of short stories. Quite a departure from our college days."

Aditi laughed at the image of Ajay, a fashion and literary maven, forming in her mind. "Wow, that's unexpected. Good for him."

"The book's on Amazon. I'll send you the link," Carol offered, keen to support her classmate-turned-author.

"Great. I'll order it," Aditi responded.

As Aditi's flight is announced, Carol bid her goodbye. "Take care, Aditi. Safe travels, and I'll see you soon."

Hanging up, Carol sat back, a sense of accomplishment mingling with the nostalgia of reconnecting with old friends.

31

Deja Vu

During a leisurely afternoon drive on Mumbai's Worli Seaface, Carol found herself immersed in a blend of music and tranquillity, her workout's afterglow evident on her flushed face.

"Where is the sea?" Carol wondered, her view dominated by concrete and construction that obscured what once was Mumbai's defining vista.

The Haji Ali dargah, set against the sea, was connected to the mainland by a slender, rocky, kilometre-long causeway that was usually submerged at high tide and perilously engulfed by waves in turbulent weather.

Mumbai's reclamation projects, which began in the 18th century, transformed the seven islets that were then Mumbai into a unified landmass, shaping the city and creating iconic landmarks like Marine Drive, Nariman Point and Cuffe Parade, among others.

"Nariman had a point, and we're on it!" declared the affable Air India Maharajah, once shouting this from the rooftop of his iconic Air India building at Nariman Point in south Mumbai. For decades, the hoarding, its updates keenly awaited and read by pedestrians and motorists along Marine Drive, has delighted Mumbaiites with its subtle humour and puns.

Khursheed Framji Nariman, also known as Veer Nariman, was a fiery lawyer, a stalwart of the Indian National

Congress, and city mayor in 1935. In the 1920s, Nariman took a stand against corruption, leading protests against British administrators and engineers for mishandling an ill-advised Backbay reclamation project.

Termed "reclamation" as an ironic nod to the sea's encroachment, these efforts involved filling the ocean with debris and stone. These projects, both old and new, had significantly altered the city's coastline.

Unhappy witnesses to this urban sprawl were the once ocean-front Art Deco buildings with evocative names such as Seaview, Seabreeze and Seawind, now offering a front row view of concrete jungles, tinged occasionally with the stench of urban avarice.

Nariman had a point.

"Guess that Mumbai exists only in memory now," Carol lamented.

Her train of thought was interrupted by her car's audio system, announcing an incoming call.

"Heyy, Aditi," Carol trilled.

From a poolside, clad in a radiant summer dress, her hair still damp from a refreshing swim, Aditi responded with equal cheer. "Heyy, Carol. How are you?"

"All good. Just heading home from the gym," Carol shared, navigating the sparse traffic with ease.

Aditi shifted the topic to something that had been occupying her thoughts. "I got Ajay's book on Kindle recently and started with the first story."

"Oh, nice. How is it? I have yet to start. No time, yaar, with all this reunion tamasha," Carol admitted.

"It's quite well-crafted, but Carol, there's something oddly familiar about it." Aditi elaborated.

Carol, intrigued, prompted her for more details. "Really? Does it recount tales from our college days?"

"No, nothing of the sort. It revolves around the unlikely friendship between a young man and an old beggar woman," Aditi clarified. "Yet, as I read, I couldn't shake off this feeling of déjà vu."

Carol urged Aditi to delve deeper. "That's interesting. What about it felt familiar?"

Aditi explained, a sense of the past washing over her. "Remember my stint at the Pune City Daily after college? I illustrated short stories sent in by readers."

Carol acknowledged the memory, "Vaguely, yes."

As Aditi paced by the poolside, a few heads turned to glimpse the lissom figure.

"Carol, I remember a short story I illustrated for that Pune daily right after college. It was written by someone claiming to be a cop from Mumbai. The story...it was about a unique friendship. Oddly enough, when I read Ajay's book, it felt so familiar."

"Go on," Carol said.

"Back at the newspaper that summer, as an illustrator, I had to dig deep into the story for the illustrations. I exchanged a few emails with this guy for an author profile and story background. And he mentioned visiting Pune," Aditi recounted.

Carol couldn't help but jest, "He didn't propose to you in those emails, did he?"

Aditi's response was swift and sharp. "No, Carol, nothing like that. He suggested we meet since he was coming to Pune. He said it would help with the illustrations."

Carol teased Aditi about the undercurrents of a blossoming romance, sparking momentary frustration from Aditi.

"Shut up, yaar! Listen, or I am going to hang up," Aditi retorted.

Carol quickly acquiesced, "Okay, okay."

Aditi continued, "I believed the meeting could provide better insights for my illustration," she explained. "Plus, I was contemplating a career in the Civil Services, even back then."

"You were a woman with a plan. You were born with a plan in your hand!" Carol exclaimed.

Mildly irked by Carol's jesting tone, Aditi clarified her stance. "I wanted insights into a Civil Services career, so I agreed to the meeting."

Carol couldn't resist a final jab, "A date, you mean? Sorry, go on."

Aditi brushed off the comment. "We scheduled a meeting in our safe haven, Vaishali. I didn't know the guy, so I was cautious. The meeting was set for a few days later," she explained, the seriousness of her tone inviting no further jests.

The anticipation built as Carol inquired about the outcome of the meeting.

"The guy did not turn up. I waited for an hour and left," Aditi revealed.

"What an anti-climax, yaar!" said Carol.

Aditi then detailed her attempts to reach out to the elusive author. "I emailed him asking why he didn't show up. There was no response, so I sent a couple more emails informing him his story wouldn't be published due to the lack of response. I think the emails bounced," she said.

Carol noted, "So you never met him."

Aditi confirmed, "No. We immediately dropped the story and picked up another. We did not want to waste time on this guy."

Carol, her curiosity still alight, asked. "So, what's the relevance of all this now? Where does Ajay Rawal fit in?"

Aditi's revelation came as a bombshell. "It's the same story, Carol. The same one I was supposed to illustrate all those years ago. It's in Ajay's new book," Aditi said. "Everything adds up. The Mumbai connection, the author's absence, and the emails. It has to be Ajay."

"What?" Carol gasped, her mind racing to connect the dots Aditi was laying out.

Aditi pressed on, her conviction clear. "The story, it's almost the same. I can't remember all the details from back then but the essence, the twist in the tale, all of it is too unique to be a coincidence. I'm absolutely sure of it."

Carol was trying to digest this information. "So, you're suggesting Ajay plagiarised the story? Is that it?"

Aditi paused, weighing her words carefully. "That crossed my mind, yes. But there's more to it. According to the introduction in Ajay's book, he claimed to have written this story around 1998."

Carol sat in stunned silence, the revelation striking her hard. "But why? Why would Ajay do something like this? And keep it a secret for so long?"

The pieces began to fall into place for Carol, but the revelation did not sit comfortably. "That's... that's incredible. And bizarre. So, you think Ajay was the one pretending to be this cop from Mumbai all along?"

"I'm convinced it was him," said Aditi. "The missing cop, the Mumbai link, the unreturned emails, his knowledge of Vaishali. It all points to Ajay."

Carol was shaken, her voice barely above a whisper. "My God... Ajay? Why would he do such a thing?"

"I don't know," Aditi sighed, her voice softening. "Maybe it was a prank, or perhaps he wanted to publish anonymously. Who knows?"

Carol pondered the implications. "So, Ajay was the mysterious author all along?"

Carol couldn't help but chuckle at the memory, taking a slight detour from the unfolding mystery. "You know, Aditi, Ajay had quite a crush on you back in college. I thought I mentioned it to you at some point."

Aditi's response was light-hearted, brushing off the revelation. "Who remembers all that, Carol? It was college; crushes came and went like seasons."

Carol, however, couldn't resist elaborating. "But Ajay's was different. You had your fair share of admirers, sure. But he was part of our gang. Just too timid to ever say anything. You were this formidable force, confident and unattainable. And Ajay? Well, he was the quintessential introvert, a nerd who found solace in his books and studies rather than the social maze of college life."

Aditi listened, her curiosity piqued despite her initial dismissal. "And you think this...this...crush he had is why he concocted the whole AK Louis scenario?"

Carol's voice carried a mix of conviction and speculation. "Think about it. Everything fits. The way he never approached you directly in college, his constant silent observation from the sidelines. And then, this story – his story – mysteriously finds its way to you under the guise of someone else. If that's not indicative of a college-time crush, I don't know what is."

Aditi paused, the pieces of a decades-old puzzle starting to align in her mind. "It's bizarre, Carol. To think, after all these years, that prank, if we can call it that, has come full circle."

Carol suggested a course of action. "We should confront him, Aditi. Not for the prank but for the silence that followed. For the story left untold."

Aditi, however, attempted to defuse the situation with her characteristic indifference. "I'm not upset, Carol. It was a lifetime ago." After a brief pause, she added, "But...yes, maybe it's time we had a little chat with Ajay. Clear the air, for old times' sake."

Carol, now determined to confront Ajay, asked, "What do you think we should do?"

A few days later, on a wet morning, raindrops streaked the windows of a luxurious living room. Aditi lounged on her plush couch in her Birmingham apartment, legs tucked beneath her, sipping tea while watching a movie on the large screen TV. A plate of bajjis jostled for space on the coffee table cluttered with documents.

Romeow, a British Longhair, perched on the back of the couch, eyed the plate intently, ready to pounce the moment his human gave him an opening.

"Don't even think about it, Romi. Down!" Aditi's command had no effect on the feline.

Aditi then gently swept Romeow down into her lap. With a mischievous glint, she clutched her phone and began dialling. A gentle purr emanated from Romeow as he settled comfortably.

"Carol, it's me," Aditi said to her friend.

"Hey, Aditi. How are you? How's the weather?" Carol asked.

Aditi looked at the endless rain outside and answered cryptically, "English!"

"That bad, eh?" Carol responded with a chuckle. "It's warm and sunny here in Mumbai. And lovely..."

"Okay, stop. You can gloat later," Aditi interjected. "Listen, it's about Ajay. Just picture this…" Aditi started, her voice teeming with excitement, "a scenario so intense, so dramatic, it would make Bollywood writers jealous. And dear Ajay? The unsuspecting protagonist in our little script."

Carol, nestled among her cherished collection of novels in her den, perked up. "You always had a flair for the dramatic, Aditi. I'm all ears," she said.

"We concoct an elaborate ruse," Aditi continued, pacing her room with intensity. "It must be set in motion on the night of the reunion and play out the next morning…"

She then detailed the plan, her voice low and conspiratorial.

Carol's laughter rang out as Aditi's animated narration drew to a close. "Wow! That's diabolically brilliant, Aditi, right out of a Bollywood showdown. Just the catchy title and dance sequence are missing! But are you sure about this? It's quite an undertaking."

Aditi nodded, even though Carol couldn't see her. "Yes, I know it's bold. But think about it, Carol. It'll be a lesson he won't forget."

Carol, now fully caught up in the spirit of the scheme, agreed. "Right, Aditi. It's daring, but let's go for it."

"Perfect, Carol," Aditi responded. "Indeed, a Sridevi-inspired Nagin dance before the climax will be the perfect touch to this revenge saga."

"You better start practicing the moves." Carol teased, the haunting, hypnotic melody of a snake charmer's been already playing in her ears.

PART 4

Resolution

32

Amazing Again

Life seemed to have come to a standstill in the usually bustling Fergusson College canteen.

Aditi stood towering, fork in hand, her words slicing the air with venom. "I am going to take those twenty-five years away from you and your family. That's only fair, don't you think? I lost twenty-five years of my life because of you," she declared, her eyes burning with a fury that set Ajay's heart racing.

Ajay, panic-stricken, accidentally sent a glass of water crashing to the floor. "What...do you mean?" he stammered, the colour draining from his face as Aditi's intentions became terrifyingly clear.

Aditi raised the fork above her head with a sinister smirk, poised to strike. Ajay shrieked and cowered desperately for safety, arms raised protectively over his head as he ducked beneath the table.

The canteen fell silent, tension thick in the air.

Peering out from his makeshift shelter, Ajay saw Aditi, Viru, Carol and Shehnaz looking down at him, their expressions unreadable. "Viru, Shehnaz, Carol...quick, do something! Why are you all just standing there?" he pleaded, bewildered by their inaction.

To his utter astonishment, laughter erupted from the group. The tension broke like a dam, and the waiters joined in, their smiles wide. They decided it could not be serious if people at the table were laughing.

"What is happening?" Ajay asked, utterly confused.

Carol, barely containing her glee, called out to him. "Mr. AK Louis, tough guy, come out from under the table. It is safe." Ajay, still unsure, found solace in Shehnaz's comforting smile as she extended a hand to help him up.

"Shehnaz?" he questioned.

"Yes, Ajay, it's fine, come out. We will explain," she reassured him.

As Ajay emerged, shaken and drenched in sweat, he glared at Aditi, eyeing the fork that sat innocuously on the table. "Aditi...she attacked me...not safe," he muttered, trying to comprehend the scene before him.

The laughter continued, echoing off the canteen walls. With a playful glint in her eye, Aditi assured him, "Well, Mr. AK Louis...Ajay. You are safe. Trust me."

But just as Ajay began to let his guard down, Aditi's hands reached up, prompting him to recoil instinctively.

Aditi grasped the edges of what everyone believed was her dishevelled, grey hair. With a flourish, she pulled off the wig, revealing her luscious hair beneath, cascading down her shoulders in waves.

The group watched, spellbound, as Aditi transformed before their eyes. Gone was the forlorn, defeated figure they had been confronted with moments ago.

In her place stood the vibrant, stunning Aditi they remembered, her eyes still lined with kohl, now adding an enigmatic charm to her radiant face.

Carol turned to Ajay with a grin, saying, "Ajay, meet the real Aditi."

Ajay's jaw dropped in astonishment as he struggled to piece together the unfolding events.

"What…do…you…mean, real Aditi?" Ajay managed to stutter.

Carol's smile widened as she leaned in, ready to unravel the elaborate ruse. "Karma has a way of catching up, Ajay. Pranks aren't your exclusive domain, you see," she quipped.

Ajay's bewildered gaze shifted between Carol and Shehnaz. The latter offered a comforting smile, her involvement in the scheme now clear. "It was all good fun, Ajay," Shehnaz added gently.

"So, this was all a setup? The stories of Aditi's downfall, her attack…all just to teach me a lesson?" Ajay asked, a reluctant smile beginning to form as he acknowledged the brilliance of their revenge.

"Yes," Carol confirmed, her smile blending mischief and satisfaction. "Indeed, Ajay, the entire thing, from the tale of Aditi's ruin to the attack, was nothing but a prank. And you must admit, we got you good."

Ajay managed to stutter out a single word, "Why?"

Now free of disguise, Aditi answered with a hint of retribution, "Why? You ask, why? Because, Ajay, it's tit-for-tat, even if it took twenty-five years to serve it back."

She glanced around at the group before she added, "We owe you a detailed explanation, of course. But before we dive into that, I need a moment to freshen up." With those words, Aditi excused herself and headed toward the washroom.

Ajay, still apprehensive, turned to Carol and said, "I am still a little confused."

Carol, keen on fresh air and a change of scenery, said, "Let's step outside, shall we? It's rather warm in here." Her amusement was evident as she glanced at Ajay, adding, "And, Ajay, you're sweating like a pig!"

She waved to the waiter, "Could we have some tea outside, please? And some cold water for sir here; he has had quite a scare."

As the old gang stepped out from the stifling air of the canteen to the cool shade provided by the old, familiar tree, the scene couldn't have been more nostalgic.

"We always knew about the AK Louis prank you pulled, Ajay," Carol began.

Ajay, recovering, feigned innocence and asked, "What prank?"

Carol's reaction was a tad derisive. "Oh, come off it, Ajay. The AK Louis story. Ring any bells?"

There was a moment's pause, a silent concession from Ajay. "So, you and Aditi knew about it all along?"

"Not quite," Carol clarified. "Aditi filled me in a few weeks back when she stumbled upon your story in your new book when she was in the UK. Imagine our surprise."

Still grappling with the revelation, Ajay asked, "Aditi is in the UK? She does not live in Pune?"

"Exactly!" Carol exclaimed as if a significant point had been made. "Everything I told you and Shehnaz about Aditi's life being ruined, the meltdowns – it was all fake, Ajay."

The realisation dawned on Ajay slowly. "So, Aditi never really fell apart because of AK Louis? She never stayed back in Pune, spiralling down?"

Carol's response was immediate. "Oh, Ajay. Never. All of it was made up. For your benefit."

As Ajay absorbed this, he sought more clarity. "And Aditi's actual life?" he ventured, curious.

"She's thriving, Ajay – the deputy head of mission in the Indian High Commission, UK. Your little pretence didn't throw her life off-course," Carol informed him.

"But you had me convinced," Ajay protested, remembering his sleepless night, pondering Aditi's fate.

Carol's hearty laughter echoed around them. "That was the plan, Ajay. To give you a taste of your own medicine. And I must say, we executed it perfectly."

Viru chimed in, grinning broadly. "It was brilliant, wasn't it? You should've seen your face, Ajay!"

Ajay, now fully aware of the extent of their plot, could only respond with a half-hearted "Get lost," though he was visibly relieved.

As Aditi stepped back into their midst, the transformation was complete. The poised, confident Aditi replaced the dishevelled and intimidating figure from the canteen they all remembered.

"Caught up on the whole saga?" Aditi asked. "Any other skeletons in your closet, Mr. Ajay Rawal? Now's the time to come out with them."

Her sudden warmth as she embraced Ajay took him by surprise. "Good to see you, Ajay," she said softly, then turned to Shehnaz with a smile. "And you must be Shehnaz. Let's make proper introductions, shall we? The one from earlier hardly counts."

Shehnaz, still laughing from the turn of events, greeted Aditi warmly. "Pleasure to meet you, Aditi. And to think the person we met earlier seemed so vicious!"

Ajay watched in stoic silence as Shehnaz and Aditi got acquainted, his mind a whirlwind of shock and shame. He stared blankly at them, laughter and chatter blending into a distant hum.

"Ajay, are you okay?" Shehnaz's voice broke through his daze, her eyes filled with concern.

He forced a smile. "Yeah, just thinking about the canteen and old times."

Shehnaz nodded, accepting his answer, though her eyes lingered on him.

Meanwhile, his friends continued their conversation, oblivious to the turmoil inside him. Ajay clenched his fists in anger, his thoughts racing. Did they think this was the right way to reconnect after twenty-five years?

He considered confronting them but quickly dismissed the idea. Not here, not now, he thought, glancing at Shehnaz. The last thing he wanted was to precipitate something and expose her to unpleasantness. This is not how he wanted his long-held desire to involve Shehnaz in this slice of his past to play out.

Taking a deep breath, he joined the conversation, his voice steady despite the hurt beneath the surface. "The chai was always the best here in this canteen," he said inconsequentially.

"Huh? Yes," uttered Viru absently.

A little calmer, Ajay turned to Aditi and, in as casual a tone as he could muster, asked, "So, Aditi, what's your post-college journey been like?"

Aditi played along with the narrative they had all been part of moments earlier. "Well, after the heartbreaking ordeal with AK Louis, I was a complete wreck. I took to alcohol and drugs and directed my anger at every man I met. My life was in shambles, really," she said, her eyes twinkling.

"Okay, okay, enough with the act," Ajay interjected, his tone now light. "What did you really do after college?"

"St. Stephen's, Delhi," Aditi began. "Followed by a leap into the Civil Services exams – cracked it in one go. And here I am, in the Indian Foreign Service."

Ajay couldn't help but marvel at her accomplishments. "As effortlessly as everything else you did back then, huh?"

Carol prodded Aditi to reveal how she had connected the dots between the prank and Ajay's recent literary endeavour.

Aditi explained, "Reading the first story in your book, Ajay, brought back memories of a similar story from twenty-five years ago when I was with the *Pune City Daily*. It couldn't have been a coincidence. Everything pointed to you; the story's timeline mentioned in your book's introduction matched." Gleefully, she added, "And, of course, Vaishali!"

"That's it, the unmistakable Vaishali connection!" Carol exclaimed as though their old haunt still wielded some influence over their fate.

Aditi continued, "Your enthusiasm for Vaishali as our meeting spot, despite AK Louis' supposed unfamiliarity with Pune, was a dead giveaway when I thought about it."

Viru was astonished at Aditi's recall. But Aditi clarified, "It wasn't recall, Viru. I found those old emails in an account I hadn't used in ages."

Ajay, now fully understanding the breadth of the ruse, could only marvel at the serendipitous way his long-forgotten story had led to this moment.

Carol couldn't resist a final dig. "Karma's a bitch, Ajay," she said, laughing. "And Aditi, your acting in there was Oscar-worthy. I was half-convinced you'd actually snapped!"

"Yeah," Ajay agreed, looking at Carol. "And you, Carol, your storytelling last night had me completely fooled. It gave me a sleepless night. I suppose I had it coming."

"Hey, Aditi," Carol suddenly remembered. "What happened to that Sridevi Nagin dance you were supposed to do? Sway and slither across the canteen floor!"

Aditi responded with a hearty laugh.

"What!" Ajay exclaimed. "That's all that was needed. Snake dances, exorcists, and haunting music would have driven me around the bend. Thank God for small mercies!"

Then his face suddenly twisted into a menacing scowl, his glare at Shehnaz so intense that it seemed he was about to unleash wrath upon her.

"SHEHNAZ!! Did you know about this? Laughing after that 'attack' – were you in on this from the start?"

Shehnaz clarified, seeking to soften the blow, "No, Ajay, it wasn't planned from the start. Carol filled me in right after we got to the college this morning."

Ajay pressed, "And you just went along with it?"

Shehnaz responded with a hint of justification, "Why not? It seemed as harmless as the prank you played."

Viru, seizing an opportunity to rub it in, interjected, "Plus, it had that Bollywood drama angle to it!"

Ajay's gaze slowly and deliberately shifted to Viru. "And you, Viru? When did you find out?" he probed.

Viru, caught in the spotlight, shrugged with an uneasy chuckle. "This morning, yaar. These conniving girls roped me into it. Honestly, I didn't want to be part of their scheme."

Viru, who could never resist college-era theatrics, threw his arms wide dramatically.

"*Tu mera bhai hai yaar. Ek hi thali se khana khaya tha hostel mein,*" he said, declaring loyalty.

Ajay, unamused by the dramatic display, snapped back. "*Faltu flimi dialogues chod, gaddaar saala.* Traitor! You would have been the first to say yes," he accused, half in jest.

Turning to the orchestrators of the elaborate ruse, Ajay demanded, "Who was the mastermind? Aditi? Carol?"

Aditi and Carol exchanged glances before Carol admitted with a mix of pride and mischief, "Alright! The idea was mine. Aditi was hesitant at first, but I managed to convince her. And, of course, Aditi was the genius behind the entire narrative – from the supposed dark days after college to the rehab saga and the canteen showdown. Her storytelling and script were absolutely brilliant."

Carol couldn't help but imitate Aditi's poignant lines. "*All I wanted from life was a career, marriage, children, happiness...I lost twenty-five years of my life because of you...I am going to finish you, Ajay...*"

As their laughter filled the air, Viru applauded Aditi's knack for drama. "You've got a real talent for storytelling, Aditi! What imagination!"

Aditi responded modestly, "The idea just struck me out of nowhere. Maybe it's all the movies I've watched?"

Still basking in the aftermath of their successful prank, Carol boasted, "We should consider a career in Bollywood. The deception, the drama – it was perfect!"

Eager to preserve the moment, Viru hinted at having captured the event on video, much to Ajay's chagrin.

Ajay conceded, with a sigh, "It seems I can't trust anyone these days. Not classmates, not hostel buddies, not even my wife."

Seizing the moment for one last jest, Aditi quipped, "Especially not Mr. AK Louis, IPS."

Though Ajay's hurt lingered, he broke free to acknowledge a more intense feeling. "Deep down," he confessed, "I'm relieved. Aditi, I'm glad you're still the old amazing Aditi."

Aditi brushed off the compliment with a modest, "Come on, Ajay! I am just me."

Ajay ventured into more personal territory, eager to shift the conversation from the recent revelations. "So, Aditi, tell us about your family."

Aditi's face lit up with the mention of family. "Well, my husband Venu is an industrialist from Chennai. He works in the EV battery and components business and sells to Indian and global EV manufacturers."

"Kids?" enquired Ajay.

"We have a son who's currently doing his Master's in automobile engineering in Germany," she shared, her voice laced with pride.

"Sounds wonderful. EVs – that's where all the action is!" Ajay responded. "I wish Venu had come with you to Pune."

"In fact, Venu will be joining us today at Vaishali. He's just landed from Chennai and is on his way there," Aditi revealed.

"That's great! I can't wait to meet him," Ajay said.

After a brief reflective pause, Ajay added, "Just one last thing, Aditi."

Cocking a curious eyebrow, Aditi asked, "What, Ajay?"

Recalling Shehnaz's advice about closure from the previous evening, following the reunion, Ajay said, "I hope you have forgiven me for that old prank. It was wrong," he admitted, his apology lingering between them while the others all looked towards Aditi.

Aditi regarded him briefly, her expression unreadable, before her features softened into a smile. "Thanks, Ajay. I appreciate that. All good. It was a harmless prank. No one was hurt," she assured him.

Always uneasy with overly emotional exchanges, Viru decided it was time to change the subject. "Okay, now it's Vaishali time. Let's go. Last stop, Vaishali," he announced, eager to relive the lighter moments of their college days at their favourite hangout.

33

Older and Wiser

As the group settled into Sheetal's familiar and welcoming atmosphere, the sit-out area in Vaishali, the tension that had dominated earlier, seemed to dissipate in the warmth of the afternoon sun.

Aditi tapped a glass with a spoon to gather everyone's attention and raised a toast. "Cheers to all of us! And a special thanks to Shehnaz for joining us and being such a sport. She's like one of us," she said, her smile inclusive and warm. "We owe you an apology, Shehnaz, for keeping you in the dark yesterday and dragging you into this prank. We wanted to make a full and proper impact."

Shehnaz waved off the apology with a laugh. "It's okay. Carol was so convincing last night at the party. That fake Aditi story had me completely fooled. Can you believe it? I even went on to give some behavioural psychology advice about rejection!"

Carol joined in the laughter, her shoulders shaking with mirth. "Sorry, Shehnaz. Yes, she was seriously offering us insights into prima donna behaviour, the blow to self-esteem, and how individuals seek validation from others after facing rejection. And how weak-minded people behave..." Her voice trailed off as she caught Aditi's stern glare.

Carol glanced at Aditi, taken aback by the sharpness of the glare, her eyebrows raised in quiet surprise.

Disregarding Carol's reaction, Aditi's gaze moved towards the entrance.

Her face suddenly lit up with a warm, welcoming smile.

The group's focus shifted to the entrance as a distinguished figure appeared. The man, clearly in his mid-fifties and sporting an athletic build, walked in confidently. His tailored jacket and salt-and-pepper hair enhanced his dignified presence. Aditi was the first to react, her face brightening with unmistakable happiness.

"Venu!" she exclaimed. Aditi rose from her chair to greet him with a hug. The couple's dynamic was immediately apparent; despite their age difference, they exuded the aura of a power duo, perfectly complementing each other in presence and poise.

"Everyone, this is Venu, my husband," Aditi introduced him to the group, her voice tinged with pride. "And Venu, these are the friends I've told you so much about," she continued, gesturing towards Carol and the rest of the gang.

The group watched as Venu greeted them. His deep, resonant voice filled the space as he said, "Hi, it's a pleasure to meet the infamous gang finally."

The group's interest was evident as they assessed Venu, Aditi's choice of partner. Their curiosity wasn't just about him, but how he measured up to the Aditi they knew from college – the heartthrob of many, one who had broken numerous hearts, who had a clear idea of what she wanted in a partner, and whose undeniable charisma had always set her apart.

They couldn't help but stare at the man who had captured Aditi's heart.

Venu's gaze shifted to Ajay and Viru, who were momentarily unsettled by his authoritative aura.

"So, you two are the boys," he commented, his voice carrying a touch of condescension. "Which of you is the great prankster?" he inquired, causing Ajay some discomfort. "I hear you had quite a day!"

The insecurities from his college days suddenly resurfaced despite Ajay's significant successes and accomplishments over the years, this time triggered by Aditi's partner.

After the introductions were dispensed with, Venu took his place among the group, immediately engaging in conversation, particularly with the women, who seemed charmed by his laidback sophistication.

Carol seized the opportunity to express her happiness at Venu's presence. "It's wonderful that you could join us from Chennai, Venu," she said.

Venu, with his arm affectionately draped around Aditi, responded. "Well, attending gatherings like this seems to be the only way I can catch up with my wife these days. She's off to London soon, and there's hardly any time for a detour to Chennai."

Aditi smiled and leaned into Venu.

In a hushed exchange at the far end of the table, Ajay and Viru couldn't help but revert to their youthful banter.

Viru, with a chuckle, nudged Ajay, "*Wah*! See that? *Bahut yaarana lagtai hai*! What affection! Ms. Aditi Joshi did marry an older and wiser guy!"

Ajay added, "True that. She always had an eye for the mature ones, didn't she? Got to admire her, though. She was a girl with a plan. She always knew what she wanted and went for it. Guess she ticked all the boxes with him."

Their jesting continued unabated. "Look at him. What did she see in him? He's a vintage model, isn't he?" Viru whispered, barely containing his laughter.

Ajay, glancing over to ensure their comments stayed between them, whispered back, "Ssshhh. They will hear us, *saala*."

Recalling Aditi's "shopping list" recounted so many times in the past couple of days, Ajay quipped. "He's mature, self-made, sensitive, adventurous."

Viru delivered the final verdict in his characteristic laconic style.

"Budda hai, saala!"

At the other end of the table, Carol, always the sucker for a love story, leaned forward with eager eyes. "So, Aditi, how did you and Venu meet? Who proposed to whom?"

The question hung in the air, drawing attention from the men.

Aditi and Venu exchanged glances that seemed to carry an unspoken understanding, their eyes briefly flicking towards Ajay.

Carol, quick to notice the subtle exchange, chimed in immediately. "Hey, Aditi, is there an Ajay connection here? Something to do with that old prank?"

Aditi hesitated, her gaze shifting to Venu without an immediate reply.

Carol's eyes widened, excitement rising in her voice. "OMG! I don't believe this. It must be. That day, twenty-five years ago, here at Sheetal!"

*

Aditi had just secured a table for two in Sheetal. She sat alone, her gaze sweeping over the crowd, searching for the enigmatic AK Louis.

Unseen by Aditi, Ajay lingered nervously at the entrance, peering in. He observed Aditi, a solitary figure, her eyes flitting toward the door frequently. A mix of guilt and hesitation tugged at his conscience, making him reluctant to dismantle the elaborate illusion he had crafted.

As the minutes ticked by, Ajay found himself paralysed with indecision. The fear of Aditi's potential anger or disappointment became overwhelming. Eventually, with a heavy heart, he turned away, leaving Vaishali and Aditi behind.

Meanwhile, Aditi continued to wait, her coffee cooling and becoming a silent marker of time.

Suddenly, she sensed someone approaching her table. Looking up, she saw a tall man standing there.

"AK Louis?" she asked hopefully, with a smile.

"Sorry?" he responded, clearly puzzled.

"Are you AK Louis from Mumbai? I was supposed to meet him here," Aditi explained.

"No, no," the man, seemingly in his late twenties, quickly clarified. "The steward said I could wait here for a table. He mentioned you'd be settling the bill soon."

"Oh, I'm sorry," Aditi apologised, "I thought you were someone else. Yes, I'm about to leave. You can sit here if you wish. I will be off as soon as I've paid the bill."

"Thank you," the man replied gratefully. "It's so crowded; I'd hate to lose this spot."

He pulled out a chair, sat down, offered Aditi a friendly smile, and introduced himself, saying, "Hi. I'm Venu. I am visiting from Chennai."

Still reeling from being stood up by AK Louis, Aditi introduced herself in a barely audible tone. "I am Aditi."

"I haven't had decent South Indian food since I arrived in Pune three days ago," Venu remarked conversationally.

He glanced around at the bustling crowd and a waiter serving crisp dosas at the next table, then added with a hopeful smile, "Looks like I might get lucky today."

*

Caught up in the drama of fate and destiny, Carol excitedly exclaimed, "You ran into Venu here at Sheetal twenty-five years ago, right?" She then cast an accusing gaze towards Ajay and added, "That was when you were waiting for that AK Louis guy who never showed up...so, Ajay's prank did lead to something good after all!"

Looking around Sheetal, she then asked. "Which table was it, Aditi? Where were the two of you sitting? Tell us!"

Aditi, laughing, gently deflected Carol's fanciful narrative. "Oh, Carol, I wish it were that romantic, like something from a fairy tale. But really, we came together in the usual way people do. We met at my parents' house. I wouldn't want to bore everyone with the mundane details."

"An arranged marriage, Aditi? Really? You?" Carol exclaimed, her voice brimming with surprise. "Wow, that says a lot about arranged marriages. A perfect match indeed!" she added with a playful chuckle. "Something for Gen-Z to note."

Aditi smiled, stood up, lifted her glass with a flourish, and glanced around at her friends.

"To us and Fergusson College!" she declared.

PART 5

Kismat

34

Troubled Souls

With its blend of old-world charm and bustling modern life, Pune held a secret tucked away in one of its quieter upmarket neighbourhoods – a private rehabilitation centre surrounded by well-manicured lawns.

The absence of signage and the building's exterior conveyed the impression of a well-to-do private residence with several outhouses and annexes. The solid doors and windows functioned as a barrier not just to muffle external noise but also to contain the clamour within.

On a bright morning, a luxury SUV drove up to the centre's porch. Inside the vehicle, a woman handed a sealed package to her driver. Without a word but with a clear understanding of the package's significance, the driver stepped out and briskly walked into the building.

The rehab centre lobby was a bubble of calm. Sunlight streamed through large windows, falling on the plush sofas and the reception desk, where a young receptionist multitasked, a phone cradled between her shoulder and ear. The driver approached, clearing his throat to announce his presence.

"Madam has sent this," he said tersely, placing the package on the desk. His voice carried slight irritation, born of the early hour and the task at hand.

The receptionist, momentarily placing her caller on hold, turned her attention to him. "Who is this for?" she asked.

The driver nodded towards the package. "The name and room number are there. Just read it," he said, his impatience thinly veiled.

The receptionist gave him a tight-lipped glare as she checked the package. "Oh, it's for room number 18," she said, then looked up just in time to see the driver walking away. She sighed and beckoned Manju, one of the attendants.

"Manju, take this to room number 18," she said, passing the package to him.

Manju hesitated, a flicker of apprehension crossing his face. "18? That's the violent one. They are all in the recreation hall now. From whom is this?"

"Does it matter? A lady sent it over with her driver; they've just left," the receptionist replied, nodding towards the entrance. "It could be the person who comes to see number 18 once in a while."

Within the walls of the recreation hall, a scene unfolded that was as routine to the staff as it was moving to an onlooker. The hall served as a temporary refuge for souls embroiled in their personal battles.

Tables dotted the space, serving as gathering spots for the inmates. Some were deeply engrossed in board games, while others seemed lost in their thoughts, their gazes fixed on voids only they could perceive. Nurses move through the hall, tending to needs, both spoken and silent.

In a corner, away from the rest, sat a middle-aged lady. At fifty, her demeanour was marked by the unmistakable signs of a life consumed by alcoholism.

Her shrill voice cut through the murmurs and activities, and her frustration and anger directed at the nurses. "You useless people! Why are you ignoring me, huh? Come here!"

A trainee nurse, Leela, caught off-guard by the intensity of the inmate's outburst, turned to her senior with a look of concern. "Is she alright, Sister Sandhya?" she asked.

"No one here is okay, isn't it?" Sister Sandhya remarked, a sad truth reflected in her eyes. "She is Asmita, Number 18; this is her daily drama. She's a hopeless alcoholic, in and out of this place every few months," she continued. "You go sit with her. She'll keep talking, you listen, don't speak or make eye contact. A few minutes of blabbering, and then she becomes calm."

Nurse Leela approached Asmita cautiously. She chose a spot some distance from the troubled woman, ready to lend an ear without intruding too much into her space.

35

Hyderabad Blues

Nurse Leela's nervousness was palpable as she sat before the inmate. Noticing the nurse's apprehension, Asmita commanded her attention with an intensity that left little room for objection.

"You are new here. I know what you all say about me. Do you know who I am? Do you know my story? Now, shut up and listen to my story! Understood?"

Nurse Leela, caught in Asmita's piercing gaze, could only manage a nod.

Asmita's voice softened as she delved into memories of her past. "We were a happy family: Dad, Mom, my sister, and I. My sister and I were very close, just a few years apart. Even as kids, we always had each other's backs and shared all secrets."

Asmita paused, a dreamy look in her eyes. "She was the smart one. Pretty, strong, ambitious…. she was also very competitive. I was the emotional, romantic type, happy to cruise along."

Asmita held up an old photograph of two young girls at a beach, their innocence frozen in time. "The two of us. Cute, isn't she? My baby!" Asmita smiled affectionately and kissed the photograph.

Just as Nurse Leela began to breathe easy, Asmita turned sharply and faced the nurse. "Are you even listening to me?" she demanded, her teeth clenched in sudden anger.

Nurse Leela nodded, too scared to speak.

Regaining her composure, Asmita continued. "She went to hostel in Pune after school, while I moved to Chennai around the same time to study journalism right after graduation." Her voice carried a hint of regret. "We were both away from home and each other for a few years. It was a happy family reunion when she returned home from Pune after her final exams."

*

The Joshi family gathered for dinner in the dining hall of their modest apartment in the Tarnaka area of Hyderabad, near the sprawling Osmania University campus.

Dr. Joshi was seated at one end of the table. The greying, fifty-five-year-old father was dressed in a white kurta-pyjama.

Sujay Ramakanth Joshi, a PhD in Particle Physics from Mumbai University, was a senior scientist at the National Quantum Research Institute. An accomplished scientist with numerous publications, he was a much sought-after guest lecturer at Osmania University and other scientific institutions in the city.

Dr. Joshi enjoyed igniting the minds of graduate and post-graduate students and research scholars. However, his real passion lay in opening the minds of high school students to the wonders of physics.

His weekend lectures in colony community halls were usually packed to the rafters, attracting young students and their parents, all eager to learn and explore.

A believer in a holistic approach to teaching science, especially in the formative years, he avoided early distinctions between physics, chemistry and biology. He always began with the concepts and first principles, often tracing back to the Big Bang.

He skillfully wove his narrative through the epochs, covering the expansion of the universe, the synthesis of subatomic particles, and the formation of simple to heavier atoms, stars and planets, culminating in the formation of the Earth.

He then moved on to the foundations of chemistry, organic matter, and finally, the origins of life – all framed as gradual extensions of core physics principles.

However, he stopped short of expressing his views on divinity and the existence of a god.

Many young students, now buzzing with scientific inquiry, questioned the rigid compartmentalisation of science and the prescribed syllabus in the schooling system, much to the chagrin of teachers and parents.

Mission accomplished, as far as Dr. Joshi was concerned!

Along the way, his daughter Aditi developed a keen sense of inquiry and analysis, challenging norms and doctrines in her unique manner.

At the other end of the table sat Sujay's wife of twenty-five years, Mrinal Hegde Joshi, clad in a crisp cotton saree. Their daughters, Asmita, aged twenty-five, and twenty-year-old Aditi, completed the gathering.

Mrinal was the steadfast anchor of a family brimming with idealistic and sometimes impractical members.

When Sujay, engrossed in academia, research and grand theories, had overlooked the importance of financial planning, which led to financial setbacks early in their marriage, Mrinal took firm control of the family finances. With two children in tow, she had developed a keen acumen for personal finance, *incrementally mastering the art of budgeting, saving and investing wisely. Her efforts ensured that the Joshi household enjoyed a very comfortable lifestyle.*

"The resourceful householder is far more useful than a profound philosopher" was the phrase she often used to open her sessions at the local NGO's women's Financial Literacy outreach programmes. There, she encouraged women to take control of their destinies and not be victims of circumstances.

Mrinal was a staunch believer in Hindu tradition and culture, often persuading the agnostic Sujay to participate in customs and ceremonies. He complied without complaint and even secretly enjoyed the meditative calm that sometimes followed his visits to temples with Mrinal.

Aditi's striking features were undoubtedly a gift of her lineage.

"Aditi, here's your favourite aamti, *spiced up just for you,"* Mrinal *said with a smile, handing a dish to her younger daughter.*

"Thanks, Ma, I missed all this in the hostel," Aditi replied.

"What is the use of giving you the recipes if you aren't going to cook?" Mrinal chided her.

Aditi responded, "Ma, no cooking in the hostel. It's mess food or tiffin dabbas. You know that."

Sujay chimed in, "I'm surprised your mother shared her secret recipes with you. Your mausi has been asking for them for years!" He affectionately added, "It's good to have you back, Aditi, and all four of us at the same place. We have been so scattered the last few years."

"Not for long, Dad. Aditi will be off to Delhi in a couple of weeks," Asmita pointed out.

Mrinal sighed, a mother's longing evident in her tone, "I know, she's here for just a few weeks. Aditi, you could have returned home two months ago and spent more time here. Instead, you chose to stay back in Pune after the final exams."

"I had to, Ma. I wanted to intern at a Pune newspaper and hone my sketching skills," Aditi replied, irritation creeping into her voice.

"You could have done that from home, too," Mrinal suggested, unwilling to let go of the topic.

Asmita jumped to her sister's defence, "Ma, you know sketching is her passion. Keeps her relaxed. She wanted to work on it in Pune with local artists."

"I just want to spend some time with the two of you before she goes off for postgrad. And then her job after that," Mrinal expressed, her voice softening.

"Ma, let her be," Asmita insisted.

They ate in silence for a while, relishing the food.

"Why couldn't you do your MA at Fergusson, Pune University, or Mumbai, Aditi? We have family there. Why do you have to go to far-off Delhi?" Mrinal questioned, reopening the discussion.

Aditi and her father exchanged looks and smiled. "Ma, not again; we have discussed this so many times. St. Stephen's has a great reputation and can help with Civil Services prep. You had agreed; it's all decided," Aditi explained patiently.

"Yes, Ma, don't start all over again. It's best for Aditi. And it's not easy to get into St. Stephen's; only the toppers can do so," Asmita added proudly.

Sujay, never one for confrontations at the dining table, tried to bury the discussion. "Assudhe, Mrinal. Let it be. We all agreed."

"Okay, okay. Father and daughters, all ganging up against me! I will keep quiet," Mrinal said, her tone shifting to good-humoured resignation. "There is porun-poli *from yesterday. I can heat it if you girls want to have some."*

*

A hush fell over the recreation hall at the rehab centre. Most of the inmates had retreated to their rooms, some weary from the long session and others drowsy from their medication.

As the hall emptied, Nurse Leela glanced around nervously, uneasy about being alone with Asmita Joshi. Her anxiety eased slightly as she spotted a couple of male attendants rearranging the furniture nearby.

Oblivious to her surroundings, Asmita pulled an old photograph from her pocket. It showed a younger version of herself and a man radiating happiness. Holding the photo up, she brought it close to the nurse's face, her eyes seeking a reaction.

She then peered closely at Leela, a curious blend of kindness and scrutiny in her gaze, "You are very pretty. Do you have a boyfriend? A lover?"

Her comment was followed by a gesture eerily reminiscent of Aditi's confrontation with Shehnaz in the college canteen. Asmita's finger traced the nurse's cheek, sending an involuntary shudder through the young woman.

Asmita looked down at the photograph with nostalgia and sorrow and remarked, "This is us. He was the love of my life. Marriage was on the cards."

*

After a brief discussion about Aditi's extended stay in Pune and her upcoming move to Delhi, the conversation at the dining table turned to more pressing issues.

Sujay looked up from his plate, addressing Asmita. "When will Venu's flight from Chennai land?"

"Tomorrow morning, ten o'clock," Asmita replied. "He's planning to go straight to his dealer's office from the airport and come here in the evening."

Aditi's earlier cheer suddenly faded; she sat back, her expression thoughtful.

"Okay, Asmita, remind him of the party we are having tomorrow evening," Sanjay instructed.

"Don't worry, Dad, he is not the type to forget. You know Venu," Asmita reassured him.

Mrinal chimed in. "Yes, he is so organised and always on top of things. I guess it's needed if you have to manage a business."

Asmita caught the subtle shift in Aditi's demeanour and asked, "You're unusually quiet, Aditi. It's great that Venu is here when you are. You'll have a chance to meet him before you leave."

Aditi managed a small smile but then turned towards their parents with a suggestion. "Can't we have a quiet dinner tomorrow, just Venu and us? Why call others?"

"Why not, Aditi?" Sujay's voice was full of reason. "Venu is going to be in town. Both you girls are here, and you will be off to Delhi soon. It will be good to have friends over."

Mrinal also weighed in: "Not just friends, Mausi and Uncle will be here, too. They haven't met you in ages."

Aditi's response was lukewarm. "Okay," she murmured, clearly not thrilled with the arrangement.

Asmita gave Aditi a puzzled look but held back from saying anything.

Eager to wrap up the meal, Mrinal said, "So, there's shrikand for dessert and some ice cream in the freezer. Your father and I want to go for a walk. We have a few things to discuss."

"All okay?" Asmita asked.

"Of course, sweetheart, just got to discuss the engagement and plans," her mother reassured her warmly. "You girls clear up."

"Sure. The weather is lovely, enjoy the walk," Aditi replied, keen to avoid further discussion.

*

Nurse Leela mechanically nodded and wondered where Asmita's story was going and how long she would have to sit there.

Asmita continued to unravel the tale. "That evening after dinner, I learned what had happened to her, why my sis Aditi was not her usual bubbly self after her return from Pune. Do you want to know why?"

Nurse Leela started nodding in fear, anticipating Asmita's reaction even before she finished her sentence.

"Then listen!!" Asmita yelled.

*

After dinner, with the parents out for a walk, Asmita and Aditi relaxed in the living room. Asmita, now in comfortable loungewear, applied a moisturiser while Aditi, still in her day clothes, focused on the TV. The bespectacled anchor's shrill voice and the ensuing slugfest compelled her to turn down the volume.

"Turn it off, Aditi," instructed Asmita as she got ready to have a sisterly chat after ages. "Good to have you back, sis."

"I'm happy to be home, even for a short while. So much to catch up on," Aditi said as she turned off the TV. "I didn't know you were serious about Venu," she added.

"Well, we have been together for a couple of years, so..." Asmita trailed off.

"I know, I just think the engagement and marriage could wait. You know, till you start work," Aditi suggested, sounding slightly judgemental.

"I don't want to link the two. Work will happen," Asmita replied, her voice casual yet firm.

Aditi wore a disapproving look, clearly not pleased with Asmita's relaxed attitude towards her career. "It's been six months since you finished your diploma in journalism. You haven't even applied for a job. Do it now, at least. Don't overthink," she advised, slightly irritated.

"You know me, Aditi, I take my time. And I don't want to deal with too many things simultaneously. Engagement, planning, marriage, new job..." Asmita's voice was calm, and her decision was clear.

"Okay. I would have approached it differently, that's all. Your priorities will change after marriage, and then the job goes out of the window." Aditi replied.

Asmita, disliking the tone, looked at Aditi silently as she wondered how to end the discussion.

"*Whatever suits you! It's your life!*" *Aditi added rather curtly.*

"*Aditi! Please don't talk like that to me! What's the matter with you? You have been on edge all evening, sulking,*" *Asmita observed.*

"*Huh? I was not sulking,*" *Aditi responded defiantly.*

"*Yes, you were. You sulked at dinner. Did not want a party tomorrow, even though Venu is coming,*" *Asmita pointed out.*

Aditi remained silent; her mood was affected by more than just family plans.

"*Mom and Dad are so excited. There is much to celebrate. You topping college, admission into St. Stephen's, Venu in town...and our upcoming engagement,*" *Asmita listed, trying to lighten the mood.*

"*It's not like you to sulk,*" *she added, shaking her head in mild reproof.*

"*Asmita, don't get me wrong,*" *explained Aditi.* "*I am happy that Venu is here and that I will finally get to meet him. I am not so thrilled about meeting the rest. The small talk, the inquisitive questions about marriage!*"

"*That's hardly a reason to sulk! That's it? Nothing else? Aditi?*" *Asmita probed further.*

"*Nothing. Let it be,*" *Aditi responded, her voice low, a clear sign that she was withholding something.*

"*You can't fool me, Aditi. I can sense it. Tell me, sis,*" *Asmita urged.*

Aditi was about to say something, then checked herself and remained silent.

"*Is it something from Pune? Or someone? Did you stay back because of that?*" *Asmita guessed, her intuition sharp.*

"NO! I did not stay back for anyone; it was just my internship. Stop it, Asmita. I don't want to talk about it now," Aditi responded vehemently.

"So, something is bothering you! Tell me, and you will feel better," Asmita persisted, her voice soothing, trying to break through her sister's defences.

Aditi remained silent and reflective, making it obvious now that she was troubled.

"A guy? A boyfriend?" Asmita asked.

Aditi responded with a barely perceptible nod that did not escape her sister.

"Oh my God! You have a boyfriend! Wow! Who is he?" Asmita exclaimed.

"No! It's not that!" Aditi snapped back.

"Then what? Oh, did you break up with him?" Asmita persisted.

"Stop it, Asmita! Stop! You don't know anything," Aditi lashed out.

"You are agitated and obviously hurting. Take a deep breath and relax. I will get you some water," Asmita said, her tone calming as she headed to the kitchen.

Returning with a glass of water, she sat beside Aditi on the couch, waiting patiently for her sister to drink and calm down.

"Tell me," she urged gently once more.

Aditi, now calmer, began to open up.

"There was this guy. I was in touch with him for several weeks," Aditi started, her voice hesitant as she delved into her story.

"He was an IPS officer and author from Mumbai. A fascinating personality," she continued.

"An IPS officer from Mumbai? So, not a classmate from college?" Asmita asked.

"No," Aditi replied.

"He must have been a few years older than you," Asmita inferred.

"Twenty-eight or so," Aditi confirmed.

"Hmmm. Okay. So, what happened?" Asmita probed.

"We never met. Just corresponded over email. I...I..." Aditi hesitated, struggling with her emotions.

"What, Aditi?" Asmita urged.

"I... I had developed feelings for him. He seemed very mature and self-made and took on a lot of responsibility for his ailing parents. Asmita, I have never spoken of this to anyone!" Aditi confessed, her voice breaking with emotion. "Not even my close friend from college, Carol."

"That is why I am here, Aditi. To hear you, to help you," Asmita reassured her.

"I know. This guy and I corresponded for a few weeks. I sensed that he was interested in me, too. He said all the right things. The story that he wrote showed great depth and conviction. I... I fell in love with him!" Aditi admitted, covering her mouth with her hands as a range of emotions crossed her face, which was now flushed red.

"Oh God, I can't believe I told you that! I feel so vulnerable," she then whispered, her voice quivering.

"Don't be silly. It's me, sis. Who else are you going to tell?" Asmita comforted her, her words tender. "What's his name?"

"AK Louis," Aditi replied.

"So, when did you finally meet him?" Asmita asked.

Aditi's eyes were moist; she was clearly on the verge of tears.

"That's the thing, Asmita. The guy did not show up for our date. He dumped me just like that! Not a word since," Aditi revealed, now breaking into tears.

"Oh Aditi, I am sorry. What a jerk!" Asmita consoled her, holding her comfortingly.

Aditi and Asmita sat together in a quiet, heartfelt exchange. As the conversation deepened, Aditi broke down, her sobs growing hysterical. Asmita held her gently, providing solace as her sister cried her heart out.

After a while, the tears subsided, and Aditi, though calmer, remained distressed.

"Come on, Aditi. It is alright. He was not the right guy for you," Asmita soothed.

"Why did he have to do this to me? Why, why?" Aditi sobbed again.

"It's all for the best. Isn't it good that you found out now and not later?" Asmita reasoned, trying to provide some perspective.

Aditi was not to be consoled and sobbed harder.

"He...he seemed like such a decent chap. Why are men like this, Asmita?" Aditi cried.

Asmita put her arm around Aditi, drawing her close. Aditi rested her head on her sister's shoulder, crying her heart out.

Suddenly, the doorbell rang, breaking the moment.

"Mom and Dad are back from their walk. Get up and go to your room. Shower and change into something comfortable. Shall I get you something hot to drink?" Asmita offered.

Aditi shook her head, wiped her face, and quickly headed to her room.

36

Venu

"I was heartbroken," Asmita confessed to Nurse Leela, her eyes moistening. "To see my baby sister so sad...my Aditi. She had never faced adversity before." Her voice trembled with rising anger as she continued, "That...that guy from Pune was a complete jerk! I fucking wanted to kill him!"

After a moment, her demeanour softened as she became pensive. "I wished there was something more I could do for her. If there were any way to trade places with her, I would have gladly done it to see her smile again."

Asmita added sadly, "She didn't want Mom and Dad to know about it. All I could do was be there for her." She paused, reflecting on her own circumstances at the time. "But you see, my life was just beginning to take off. My engagement was around the corner, and I hoped all the joy and celebration would lift Aditi's spirits."

*

The living room of the Joshi residence exuded elegance, each piece of furniture and decor chosen with an eye for beauty and harmony.

The soft lighting inside bathed everything in a gentle luminescence. Vases with fresh, long-stalked flowers added a burst of nature's beauty. Crystal showpieces caught and reflected the colours of the room's lighting. The walls were adorned with a handful of vibrant abstract paintings, all creations of Mrinal Joshi herself.

The room stood ready, eagerly awaiting the arrival of the evening's guests.

Mrinal stepped into the room. Her eyes scanned the setup and rested on a slightly askew frame, which she adjusted. Turning from the room, Mrinal raised her voice slightly, calling out to her husband, "Sujay! Hurry, the drinks have to be cooled before the guests arrive."

In the bedroom, Asmita sat in front of the mirror, carefully putting on a pair of earrings and adjusting her hair. Her gaze shifted between self-admiration and critical assessment. Slightly heavier and a couple of inches shorter than her sister, Asmita exuded chic elegance.

Aditi, dressed in a simple yet elegant white salwar kameez, presented a contrasting image. Her face was free of makeup, letting her natural beauty shine through as she brushed her lustrous hair.

"How do I look?" Asmita asked, scrutinising her reflection from various angles.

"Great," Aditi responded with a playful roll of her eyes. "You've been at it for hours now!"

"Hah! Some of us have to," Asmita chuckled. She suddenly glanced at her watch and exclaimed, "It's almost seven-thirty. Venu will be here any minute now!"

"Come, then let's go to the hall and wait," Aditi urged, gently trying to coax Asmita away from the mirror.

As they approached the doorway, Asmita stopped and faced Aditi, her expression turning serious. "Listen, I want to tell you something," she said, drawing her sister's attention.

Aditi looked at her, sensing the shift in tone.

"About yesterday's discussion regarding Pune and that author guy," Asmita continued, her voice soft but firm. "Just forget everything for tonight. Enjoy the company and the party. Everything is going to be fine. Trust me." She smiled comfortingly and added, "Remember, you are Aditi. Things just fall in place for you."

Aditi nodded, her smile lacking warmth, but she acknowledged her sister's intent to comfort. Sensing the need for closeness, Asmita put an arm around Aditi and drew her in for a supportive embrace.

"I will be fine," Aditi said softly. "Tell me something more about Venu before he gets here."

At twenty-eight, Venu Dalapathi was the founder and CEO of Veda Energy, a growing business dedicated to providing innovative power solutions for small and medium-sized enterprises.

Venu had done his schooling in Namakkal, Tamil Nadu, where his father was a lower division clerk at the State Electricity Board and his mother a primary school teacher. Their middle-class values had stood Venu in good stead. A gold medallist in Electrical and Electronics Engineering from the College of Engineering, Guindy in Chennai, Venu initially joined the research wing of a leading multinational company in the electrical equipment sector.

However, the lure of entrepreneurship soon took hold, and he ventured out to establish his own electrical components manufacturing unit near Chennai.

The venture, however, was short-lived. Faced with severe production hurdles, including labour disputes and frequent power outages, the unit was compelled to cease operations within the first year.

Smarting from this early failure, Venu contemplated a return to corporate life. Yet, amidst the ruins of his failed enterprise, he spotted a golden opportunity: manufacturing captive power units tailored for small businesses. Venu and team went on to develop a compact solution featuring advanced battery technology, and Veda Energy soon established a significant presence throughout Tamil Nadu.

The stage was now set for national expansion.

Outside of work, Venu, a sprinter during his school days, had taken to marathons. He was also an active advocate for providing clean drinking water to all.

Venu crossed paths with Asmita during her internship at a Chennai daily, where she covered his manufacturing unit as a cub reporter.

Sparks had flown, and not from any of the batteries lying around the workshop.

*

Asmita hastily wiped the spittle off her mouth with her sleeve, then took a large, clumsy gulp of water, some of which spilt down onto her gown. "Even the water is awful in this rathole," she complained, gesturing vaguely at no one in particular. "You won't get away with it!"

"What are you doing here?" Asmita suddenly snapped, looking at Nurse Leela.

"I...I..." Nurse Leela stammered, taken aback by the question.

"Shut up and listen to my story!" Asmita then yelled.

Then, almost as quickly as her anger flared, it subsided, and she continued in a calmer tone, "It was a fun evening. Mom and Dad looked so happy. Venu arrived, looking as cool and handsome as ever." A touch of nostalgia softened her features. "And I was looking forward to Aditi meeting Venu. Her approval meant so much to me!"

*

As Asmita and Aditi entered the hall, they found their father, Sujay, and a young man, Venu, already there. Venu, tall and slim, rose immediately upon seeing the sisters.

Asmita approached him with a bright smile and enveloped him in a warm, affectionate hug. "Venu! I'm so glad to see you! How was your day?" she asked enthusiastically.

"It went well," Venu replied warmly, his arm lingering around Asmita as he turned to Aditi, who stood a little behind. "And you must be Aditi," he said, his smile widening.

With a playful tug, Asmita pulled Aditi closer and introduced them. "Venu, this is my little sister Aditi. Aditi, meet Venu."

Aditi rolled her eyes at being called "little sister" but extended a warm smile to Venu. "Hello, Venu. I'm glad to meet you finally," she said.

"The pleasure is all mine, Aditi," Venu replied, reaching for a handshake.

At that moment, Mrinal walked into the room and warmly greeted Venu. "Hello, Venu. It's wonderful to see you here," she said.

"Hello, Aunty. Thank you for inviting me," Venu responded with a touch of formality, adding, "You really shouldn't have taken all this trouble to throw a party."

"It's nothing, Venu," Mrinal dismissed with a wave of her hand. "Just a small informal gathering of close friends."

Sujay, meanwhile, stood up, ready to play his part as host. "You people settle down. I need to get the drinks out," he said as he walked away.

"So, Venu, how was the dealers' meeting?" Asmita inquired, linking her arm with his, eager to catch up with her fiancé.

"Hectic, Asmita. It took longer than expected," Venu explained. "There has been a spurt in demand, with all the new industrial parks coming up and the erratic power supply."

The doorbell rang, signalling the arrival of the evening's guests.

Several hours into the party, the guests were deeply engaged in conversation. Dr. Shaji Mathai, Sujay's colleague from the Labs and their neighbour, was deep in scientific discussion with Sujay, the alcohol rendering both a bit incoherent. Meanwhile, Minnie, Dr. Shaji's wife, wandered around the room, admiring Mrinal's abstract paintings and searching for nonexistent deeper meanings.

Sridhar Reddy, the President of the Rotary Club, was chatting with Asmita, persuading her to join the club. His wife, Janaki, flipping through the Joshi family album, asked, "Mrinal, is this you or Aditi? Tough to tell."

On the couch, Mrinal's cousin Abha chatted with Venu while her husband Deepak sampled the array of dishes on the dining table. Mrinal, ever the attentive host, flitted about the room. Aditi, seated next to Abha, quietly observed the lively interactions around her.

"Veda Energy. That's an interesting name, Venu," said Abha, her curiosity piqued. "Why Veda? Is it named after someone dear, or does it have a deeper Vedic significance?"

Venu just smiled as if pondering the best way to explain. "Nothing like that," he finally responded with a sheepish grin. "It's just coined from my name – Venu Dalapathi. 'Ve' from Venu and 'Da' from Dalapathi!"

"Oh, I see, very nice," Abha replied, slightly amused by her assumption of a profound origin story and the somewhat vain reality.

"Dinner is ready if anyone cares to eat," Mrinal announced, attempting to gather everyone's attention. Receiving no immediate response, she focused on the scientists engrossed in their conversation. "Sujay, Shaji! Don't you scientists talk enough at work? Sujay, please check on everyone's drinks. It seems no one's ready for dinner yet."

Sridhar Reddy stood up, lending support to Mrinal, and began herding guests toward the dining area. "Mrinal has set the table for us, folks. Let's serve ourselves first and continue our discussions over dinner and dessert," he suggested.

"Abha, Venu, girls, come on," he called out to the group.

"Uncle, guests first. We will join in later," Aditi responded graciously as Asmita rose to help her mother at the table.

With the others at dinner and the hall quiet after the evening's discussions, Aditi and Venu finally had a chance to get acquainted.

"Venu, I hope you are enjoying the party," Aditi said.

"Oh, yes. A nice mix of people. I had an interesting discussion with Mr. Sridhar Reddy about the Rotary Club and drinking water projects. I am considering sponsoring some projects in my hometown, Nammakal," Venu shared, adding, "Though I couldn't grasp what Dr. Shaji was saying about Vedas, energy and quantum phenomenon, and their interconnectedness." With a chuckle, he said, "He probably thinks I am a Vedic scholar!"

"You obviously didn't think 'Veda Energy' through when you named it that!" Aditi laughed, with Venu joining in.

"Then again, I do need to delve into Quantum phenomena and applications for Energy," Venu mused thoughtfully.

"Yes, energy, that is the future," Aditi agreed.

"You bet," Venu nodded. "I see clean energy, or green energy as some call it, coming into focus. People are becoming more conscious about the environment."

"I agree. Fossil fuels are not sustainable in the long run. The economics won't work out. The Law of Diminishing Returns applies there, too, apart from environmental considerations. Sooner or later, there should be a sustainable alternative," Aditi commented.

"Very perceptive, Aditi. That's exactly how we see it at Veda Energy. We're exploring options in that area, looking for some tie-ups with research centres here and in the USA," Venu shared.

"Energy Economics and Energy Finance is a promising area of study. I was reading an article..." Aditi began, but their conversation was interrupted as Asmita plopped down on the couch between them, snuggling up to Venu affectionately.

"Mom is managing fine. The maid, Pushpa, has stayed back to help," Asmita said. Looking at the two, Asmita asked, "So what were the two of you talking about?"

"Energy Economics and Energy Finance," Venu offered helpfully, with a smile.

"What?" Asmita exclaimed. "What is that?"

Venu started to explain, but Asmita shushed him with a wave. "No, don't tell me. I won't understand it anyway," she laughed.

Aditi and Venu exchanged smiles.

"That was an interesting chat, Aditi," Venu remarked. "We should continue this discussion some other time."

"Definitely," Aditi agreed with a smile and an enthusiastic nod.

"Good," Asmita chimed in. "I have a plan."

Curious, Aditi and Venu turned their attention to her.

"Let's do dinner tomorrow. The three of us, and maybe a couple of my friends," Asmita proposed enthusiastically. "Venu, you'll get to meet my friends." With a wink at Aditi, she added, "And Aditi too."

Aditi frowned, guessing at Asmita's underlying intent.

"I'm game," Venu said, looking hopefully at Aditi. "Aditi?"

"Yep, me too," Aditi replied with a slow smile.

"Great," Asmita said, watching the guests return to the living area with plates. She hauled herself up and declared, "Come on, let's get dinner. I'm famished."

37

Bazaar Buzz

"That was a fun weekend in Hyderabad," Asmita reminisced to Nurse Leela, her voice lightening momentarily. "I made sure Aditi didn't spend time alone sulking. We went out for dinner, caught a movie, visited the old city, bought bangles at Charminar and went to the Salar Jung Museum." She paused, smiling faintly. "Venu was with us, too. He was understanding and didn't mind missing out on our private time so Aditi could feel better. It really lifted her spirits."

Watching Asmita's calm demeanour, Nurse Leela felt a twinge of anxiety, wondering when the calm would break.

Asmita continued, her voice falling into a flat drone as she recounted a story she had told many times before at the rehab centre.

*

The Charminar stands as a testament to Quli Qutb Shah's decision to shift his capital from nearby Golconda to Hyderabad.

The Qutb Shahi dynasty, a Persianate Shia Islamic dynasty, ruled the wealthy Golkonda Sultanate in Southern India in the 16th century CE. The historic city of Golconda was its capital.

Sultan Muhammed Quli Qutb Shah, the 5th Sultan of the Qutb Shahi dynasty, founded the city of Hyderabad in 1591 CE on the banks of the River Musi. The Charminar, the centrepiece of the new city, was constructed in the same year.

Hyderabad's governance underwent significant historical transformations, moving from the Qutb Shahi dynasty of the Golconda Sultanate to Mughal rule and subsequently to the Nizams of the Asaf Jahi dynasty.

This evolution transformed the region from a Sultanate into a major princely state under the British Indian Empire. It later acceded to independent India and was eventually dissolved following the reorganisation of states in 1956.

Hyderabad's urban sprawl has led to the designation of the original city areas as the "Old City," a term that conjures images of a lively and vibrant locale steeped in history.

The Charminar area of Hyderabad remains a bustling hub of activity.

On that summer afternoon, the area around the monument buzzed with the hustle of tourists, locals, street vendors, and shopkeepers. The harsh sun drove everyone to seek comfort in the shade, where juice and cut-fruit vendors did brisk business, enticing passersby with offers and promises of once-in-a-lifetime experiences.

Asmita, Venu and Aditi positioned themselves far enough from Charminar to appreciate the imposing structure in its entirety.

"It's fascinating," Venu remarked. "It's not just the grandeur of the structure itself but the vibrancy around it – with all the bazaars and people milling about – that makes it a living monument, not just some cordoned-off relic."

Venu noticed the Bhagyalakshmi Temple, a shrine attached to the southeast corner of the Charminar. 'Hmm, unusual neighbours. How did that come about?' he mused.

"*Ganga-Jamuni tehzeeb, miyan*," Aditi replied cryptically.

This coexistence of the monument and the temple is seen by some as a symbol of Hyderabad's composite culture and secular traditions and the Ganga-Jamuni tehzeeb – a syncretic fusion of Hindu and Muslim cultural elements.

However, as is universally the case with such juxtapositions, this unusual pairing has inevitably brought its share of claims and counterclaims.

As one looked around, all that was visible were people mingling peacefully in a display of harmony and unity.

"This is why I love this part of town. It's alive." Aditi reflected. "It's as if it's caught in a time warp, with its warmth, character and tradition still preserved."

"Let's get out of the sun," Asmita suggested. "I want to explore Laad Bazaar and check out the bangle stores. Aditi, want to join me? Venu, maybe you can walk around and see the Mecca Masjid and the Chowmahalla Palace."

"Not in this heat, Asmita. Let's come back another evening. How about a visit to the Salar Jung Museum? All these years in Hyderabad, and I haven't yet been there!" Aditi suggested, preferring a more culturally enriching experience over casual shopping.

"Good idea," Venu agreed. "We can escape this heat. I've heard so much about the veiled Rebecca statue at the museum. I hope it's on display."

"Guys, there's so much to see around this place; this is the real Hyderabad! I have no interest whatsoever in looking at the assorted collectables of some old nawab," Asmita declared.

"Okay," Aditi said, making a quick plan. "You finish your bangle shopping. I'll treat Venu to some Irani chai and bun *maska, and then we'll all head to the Salar Jung Museum. What do you say, Venu?"*

"Throw in a biryani, and I am all yours for the rest of the day," Venu said with a smile. "Hey, I'm cool with whatever you sisters decide. It's your city," he added affably.

38

Cosmic Connection

"After that weekend, everything seemed to fall into place," Asmita recounted. "Venu returned to Chennai with sizeable orders for Veda Energy, and Aditi went off to New Delhi for her postgrad at St. Stephen's. I was busy with the engagement preparations and considering a part-time job, just as Aditi had suggested."

She took a deep breath and closed her eyes, a moment of silence enveloping her as if she was bracing herself. Nurse Leela tensed, sensing the brewing storm.

Suddenly, Asmita's voice cracked as she screamed, banging the table, causing an empty glass to topple. "Then, life dealt me a cruel blow!"

Nurse Leela's professional instincts screamed caution, but against her better judgement, she found herself getting drawn into the saga. The details of the sisters' story and the sheer rawness of Asmita's emotions were compelling. She felt invested in their tale, curious to see how it would unfold.

Despite her fear of a fresh meltdown, the nurse leaned forward slightly. "What exactly happened?" she asked, her voice a mix of caution and curiosity.

Asmita's face was a mask of anguish as she recounted, "Venu called weeks later. They were struggling with production issues at Veda Energy, could not fulfil orders, and losing customers and revenue."

Nodding solemnly, Nurse Leela absorbed every word, a stark departure from her earlier apathy.

Asmita's voice grew bitter. "A week after that call, Venu said things were worsening, and drastic measures were needed. Then, the final blow – he said our engagement had to be postponed indefinitely because of the crisis at work. No matter how much I pleaded, he wouldn't budge. His calls became infrequent; he stopped answering calls, too."

Her voice dropped to a whisper, "After a month or so, with heavy hearts, my parents called off the engagement… and the marriage."

"I wanted to go to Chennai to talk to him," Asmita continued, her tone softening. "But Aditi and my parents dissuaded me. They thought that it was a blessing in disguise that his true nature was revealed before any formal commitments were made."

Asmita shook her head wistfully as the regret and pain of the long-ago incident washed over her. "I slowly picked up the pieces and threw myself into freelance and part-time writing," she continued, her voice growing steadier. "Aditi was relieved to see me focusing on my work."

As Asmita's voice dropped, hinting at more darkness ahead, Nurse Leela's fear grew. "After a while, I started meeting other people, taking things slow."

Abruptly, Asmita slammed her hand down again. "Four, nine, two thousand," she said cryptically, then elaborated, "April Ninth, 2000 – it's a day etched in my mind. That's when Aditi called from New Delhi."

Her voice trembled with emotion. "She had just cleared her UPSC exams and was likely to get into the IFS. We were overjoyed, crying happy tears. Then, she dropped a bombshell."

Asmita's voice broke. "She had gotten married just hours earlier in a civil ceremony in New Delhi. *'I am now Aditi Dalapathi,'* she told us, without emotion."

"*Dalapathi*. It took a minute to register. *Dalapathi!*" Asmita's voice was a mix of disbelief and betrayal.

"*'Venu?'* was all Mom could ask before the line went dead. That was the last time they spoke."

"Venu Dalapathi!" Asmita whispered, the name reopening a wound.

"Three lives were shattered that day. Four, nine, two thousand."

Nurse Leela, though fearful, felt compelled to offer some solace. "I am sorry," she said, her voice barely audible. She wanted to lay a comforting hand on Asmita's shoulder, but Sister Sandhya's earlier stern warning kept her from doing so.

"And you know what?" Asmita continued. "We later found out that Aditi and Venu had started seeing each other right after his visit to Hyderabad. The crisis at Veda Energy? It was all a ruse to push me away. They had been carrying on behind my back for weeks!"

Asmita continued in an even tone, now explaining Aditi's behaviour. "Aditi was jilted by someone she was deeply in love with back in college. That really wounded her pride. Imagine someone rejecting her!"

She paused, allowing the gravity of her words to sink in. Nurse Leela was struck by how lucid and normal Asmita sounded.

"She met my fiancé soon after her rejection. Determined not to let this guy slip through her fingers, she latched onto him instead – and eventually married him!" Asmita's tone conveyed a mix of disbelief and resignation. "She probably felt she deserved him more than I did! A meeting of minds, a cosmic connection," she added with a sneer. "…and lots of chemistry, too, I'm sure."

Her voice escalated with each word, "And the jerk, Venu, quickly switched to the smarter, prettier, younger sister! The opportunistic bastard!

"The signs were all there that weekend in Hyderabad," Asmita reminisced. She pointed at herself and added, "Just that this trusting idiot didn't see them. But then, who could have imagined?"

The rising anger in her voice made Nurse Leela nervous, prompting her to look around for the reassuring presence of the senior nurse.

From a distance, Sister Sandhya signalled her to stay put, watching closely. She had seen Asmita Joshi doing this walk down memory lane before and knew it could either end in a slump of depression or manic fury.

Asmita then reflected on the tragic consequences of betrayal by those she held dear and loved. "Their actions ruined my life – my baby sister and my fiancé! I could not deal with that. It left me heartbroken and shattered. "

Asmita reflected briefly before saying, "My parents couldn't cope with it, either. This wasn't just betrayal; it was the obliteration of our family and the dreams they had woven for it, destroyed systematically from within. Dad took early retirement, and Mom and he moved to Shirdi, spending the remainder of their lives in isolation."

She paused, her gaze piercing through the nurse, "You know, I was the weak, sensitive, simple one. You know what I wanted from life? Huh? Huh?"

Her words echoed those spoken by Aditi in the canteen "attack," a haunting similarity, though the nurse wasn't to know.

"All I wanted from life was a career, marriage, children, happiness. Isn't that what every woman desires? The life that my sister has. Instead, I have nothing...I lost twenty-five years of my life because of her and this guy."

Aditi's elaborate college reunion prank and drama, aimed at Ajay, seemed to draw on Asmita's real-life trauma.

Having witnessed her sister's rants, angry outbursts, and meltdowns over the years, Aditi had a playbook for crafting a compelling narrative that the unsuspecting Carol and the others believed to be a stroke of genius by their amazing Aditi.

Ironically, the very person who seemed to be the victim of Ajay's old prank, driven by her sense of entitlement and privilege, had deliberately triggered her own vulnerable sibling's misery.

Asmita reflected, almost to herself, "I can't blame my sister and husband, can I? It was not her fault. She was a victim, too; she told me so."

The shock and trauma of betrayal, combined with years of alcohol abuse and manipulative influence from a calculating sibling, had severely impaired Asmita's ability to reason and exercise basic judgement.

"I deserve this. I asked for it. After Aditi told me of the Pune heartbreak, I wished I could trade places with my sister, just to see her smile again," Asmita rationalised. "The universe has orchestrated this. Now, here I am, and there she is, living her dream life. It's not her fault."

Asmita paused, her eyes flickering in a sudden shift from wild intensity to calm understanding. "You know, it's strange," she said, her voice softening. "I find myself thinking that maybe Aditi didn't mean any harm. Maybe she was just...misunderstood?"

Nurse Leela raised an eyebrow but remained silent, letting Asmita continue.

"It's confusing. It's as if there are voices from somewhere else, gently telling me to see things differently."

Asmita suddenly glared at the nurse and demanded, "Do you know what my name, Asmita, means?"

Nurse Leela shook her head.

"Pride!" Asmita exclaimed, a maniacal glint in her eye. "Asmita means pride, self-respect." She pointed to herself and said, "Look at this!" and then laughed hysterically. Between her howls, she managed to spit out a few words. "What a joke! What a cruel joke!"

Asmita stopped laughing abruptly and held up their beach picture again. Her expression softened momentarily as she pondered, "She has been kind enough to pay my bills. Her husband is super, super rich. *My* Venu!" Her tone was laced with both anger and pride.

Looking lovingly at the photo, she asked, "Can I blame my sister and family? See how cute she is? She looks just like Mom. She is all I have now. It's not my sister's fault. It was this guy who dumped her; it was his fault, right?"

Nurse Leela gulped and nodded in agreement.

Asmita's tone shifted, hinting at a resolution, "Right. You know what I am going to do? I am going to find this Pune guy one day and…"

Her voice trailed off, leaving an ominous silence hanging in the air.

Nurse Leela looked askance, her wariness evident. Having witnessed Asmita's sudden mood shifts and rants over the last thirty minutes, she didn't know what to believe. Yet, there was something chillingly convincing in Asmita's tone.

"You don't believe me, hmm?" Asmita continued, reading the expression on Nurse Leela's face. Her voice was perfectly normal yet deadly serious. "I have the means to do it. And I will do it the moment I find him."

As quickly as it had begun, her agitated demeanour settled into a depressed calm. Her venting, culminating in her final threat of retribution, seemed to temporarily exorcise the raging demon inside her. Her face softened into a mask of exhaustion. The room felt quieter, as if a storm had just passed.

The air was punctuated by the footsteps as someone approached.

Manju, the attendant, came up to them, a package in hand.

"Madam, you had a visitor," he announced.

"Who? Who?" Asmita's inquiry was sharp.

"Some lady. Maybe the one…" Manju started to answer and then checked himself. He resumed, a smirk adorning his face, "The only one who visits you once in a while. But she did not stay. She left a package for you." Handing over the package, the attendant watched as Asmita snatched it from him.

Asmita dismissed the attendant with a nasty, "Get lost! Why are you still here?" She feigned a blow, causing the attendant to leave with a sneer, glad to put distance between himself and the unstable woman.

Nurse Leela, taking the cue, made a hasty retreat. The weight of the intense emotions she had witnessed pressed down on her as she left the room and headed to the balcony.

Alone now, Asmita tore into the package with feverish urgency, her fingers trembling as they unearthed a book and a note from within.

The book *Reflections* by Ajay Rawal seemed to hold the final piece of this twisted puzzle.

The note's message was chilling in its simplicity: "*Hi, Asmita. I have found the guy who did this to us. From your loving sister, Aditi.*"

Asmita gripped the book with intensity, her focus narrowing on the author's name on the cover.

Flipping it over, she directed a deadly gaze at the author's photograph on the back, her eyes piercing through the image as if to reach the person behind it.

Epilogue

Ajay and Shehnaz returned to Bengaluru a couple of days after the reunion in Pune, following a brief stopover in Mumbai to spend time with Shehnaz's sister and family. Swamped with work, pending calls and meetings, neither had the chance to discuss the eventful reunion trip. Their brief exchanges at the dining table were limited to transactional domestic matters, investment concerns and hurried calls with their children in the USA.

Only a couple of weeks later, when Ajay finally had some breathing room, the nagging thoughts about the Pune trip resurfaced. Sitting in his study, the events replayed in his mind like a relentless film reel.

Despite the upbeat conclusion, his heart still ached from the sting of Aditi and Carol's manipulation and the way their prank had unfolded. The rush of the reunion, the hectic Mumbai visit, and subsequent work pressures had not allowed him to process his feelings. But the moment he had a break from his work commitments, it hit him like a tonne of bricks.

Ajay rubbed his temples, trying to dispel the bitter thoughts that gnawed at him. The idea of Shehnaz's involvement hurt the most. He couldn't shake off the feeling of betrayal when Shehnaz joined in the prank. Her laughter echoed in his mind, mocking and cruel. Did she see him as a joke? Had she, too, been laughing at him?

Why hadn't she given him a heads-up that morning at Fergusson?

The brief interaction with Venu at Vaishali only added to his turmoil, bringing old insecurities to the fore. Ajay clenched his fists, the memory of Venu's smirk making his blood boil. It was a toxic cocktail that tormented him, the bitterness and resentment seeping deeper despite his efforts to bury them.

He had to speak to Shehnaz.

Ajay found Shehnaz in the living room, engrossed in a book. He took a deep breath, steeling himself for the conversation.

"Shehnaz, can we talk?" he asked.

She looked up and smiled. "Of course, Ajay. What's on your mind?"

Ajay sat down next to her, struggling to find the right words. "I've been thinking about the reunion...about what happened with Aditi."

Shehnaz nodded, waiting for him to continue.

"It felt like everyone was laughing at me...you too." His voice trailed off. "I am talking about how Aditi pretended to go around the bend," he added.

Shehnaz's eyes widened with surprise. "Ajay, are you still thinking about that? I admired the way you gracefully accepted it. Apparently, you haven't."

Ajay remained silent.

"No, Ajay," Shehnaz offered. "I wasn't laughing at you. I would never do that to you. I thought we were having fun. I had no idea it would hurt you like this."

Ajay sighed, the tension in his shoulders easing slightly. "It's not just that. I feel like I've let myself down in your eyes, too. Pretending to be AK Louis and all that...it was stupid. I made a fool of myself."

After a moment's reflection, Ajay added, his voice forceful. "I shouldn't have published that damn story and book! I shouldn't have told you about the prank in college! We shouldn't have attended the reunion! I feel like such a fraud. And now Aditi, Carol, everyone knows. They must be all laughing at me."

Shehnaz reached out, patting his hand. "Don't be too hard on yourself, Ajay. You didn't let me down. And their opinions shouldn't matter to you now. Look at your achievements. You are up there today."

Ajay looked into her eyes, seeking the reassurance he desperately needed. "You think so? Nothing has really changed, right?"

"Of course not, Ajay. Everything's intact," Shehnaz reassured him.

"Thank you, Shehnaz. I needed to hear that," Ajay said gratefully.

"Give it some time, Ajay," Shehnaz gently advised. "All those negative feelings and thoughts will ebb away."

Ajay could only nod.

Then, more firmly, Shehnaz continued, "Ajay, if you ask me, it's been quite an overdose of Aditi. Amazing or not."

After a brief, reflective moment, she added, "Yes, I did indulge you in your Aditi recollections at the reunion. You were, after all, getting together with your friends after twenty-five years. But enough. You need to know when to let go. Move on."

Ajay, not quite sure how to respond to Shehnaz's unexpected missive, stared at her in stunned silence.

With a tone of finality, she ended the discussion. "I will not entertain any more talk about her or the incidents at the reunion. Period."

With that, Shehnaz returned to her book.

In the dead of night, a muted sodium vapour glow enveloped Royale Woods, casting its light over the sprawling Rawal residence. The villa stood elegantly, surrounded by neatly manicured lawns and curated flower beds.

A drizzle and a soft breeze stirred the leaves of the trees near the house.

Inside the villa, silence reigned supreme. Ajay and Shehnaz, deep in slumber, were in their spacious bedroom on the upper floor, adrift in the sea of dreams that comes only in the deepest hours of the night.

Ajay had been dreaming yet again of a troubled and psychotic Aditi. Suddenly, he awoke with a start. A sound had pierced his slumber. Instinctively, his eyes darted to the foot of the bed, searching for shadows or shapes.

Finding nothing, he sought solace in their bed's cosy embrace, pulling the comforter tighter as he tried to drift back to sleep. Beside him, Shehnaz shifted, her voice a sleepy whisper, murmuring, "Hold me, Ajay." Ajay wrapped his arms around her, the remnants of his fears dissolving.

The curtains, typically motionless sentinels of the night, betrayed a subtle disturbance, a whisper of movement.

Acknowledgements

To my family and friends for their unwavering support

To my college and hostel mates who created the moments that inspired me to tell a tale

To the core members of The Writers Collective, Bengaluru, for their inputs and support

To Sheila Kumar for invaluable edits, feedback and suggestions

To my Publishing Manager Diksha Lohia and the team at Notion Press for their support

About the Author

RR Cherla is a seasoned IT industry veteran who lives in Bengaluru. He is an avid swimmer and is an alumnus of IIT Mumbai and Fergusson College, Pune.

His debut novel, "Devil's Ether" (2012), a high-tech political thriller, received favourable reviews for its prescient depiction of US intelligence agencies' surveillance activities.

Silver in the Dust, the short story penned by the elusive AK Louis in *Amazing Aditi,* is one of RR Cherla's earlier works, written almost twenty-five years ago. It can be found in *Relationship Ragas (2023)* – an anthology of short stories co-authored by RR Cherla.

www.ingramcontent.com/pod-product-compliance
Lightning Source LLC
Chambersburg PA
CBHW032018150726
47990CB00005B/2024